ADALINE FALLING STAR

☆MARY POPE OSBORNE☆

**SCHOLASTIC
PRESS**

For Will and Bailey

ACKNOWLEDGMENTS

I would like to thank the wonderful friends who read and advised me on this book:
Wilborn Hampton, Ken Whelan, Kate McMullan and Susan Sultan.
I cannot thank my editor Tracy Mack enough. Her enthusiasm, care and
guidance made our work together a pure joy. I also thank my agent
Gail Hochman for her abiding good wisdom and fantastic support.
I thank my husband Will. This book would not have been written without him;
he knew Adaline as well as I did and lovingly helped her steer her course.
And finally I thank my Norfolk terrier Bailey. She sat faithfully beside me every
day while I wrote and generously offered her advice on the character of Dog.

Scholastic Children's Books,
Commonwealth House, 1-19 New Oxford Street,
London, WC1A 1NU, UK
a division of Scholastic Ltd
London ~ New York ~ Toronto ~ Sydney ~ Auckland
Mexico City ~ New Delhi ~ Hong Kong

First published by Scholastic Inc., 2000
First published in the UK by Scholastic Ltd, 2001

Copyright © Mary Pope Osborne, 2000

Cover illustration by George Smith

ISBN 0 439 99812 3

Printed by Cox & Wyman Ltd, Reading, Berks.

10 9 8 7 6 5 4 3 2 1

☆ A NOTE ON SOURCES ☆

While my novel is a work of fiction, I'm very grateful for all the historical sources that helped me understand American frontier life in the 1840s. To single out a few from the many:

Bent's Fort by David Lavender and *The Life of George Bent* by George E. Hyde provided wonderful details about life at a trading fort. A visit to the Colorado History Museum in Denver also gave me valuable information on 1840s Colorado life.

I am indebted to *Wah-To-Yah and the Taos Trail* by Lewis Garrard, *The Story of the Indian* by George Bird Grinnell, *The Arapahoes, Our People* by Virginia Cole Trenhelm, and *The Arapaho* by A.L. Kroeber for information on the Arapaho way of life.

Kit Carson, Folk Hero and Man by Noel B. Gerson, *Kit Carson's Autobiography* edited by Milo Milton Quaife, and *Dear Old Kit* by Harvey Lewis Carter taught me about the life of the famous scout. *Fremont, Explorer for a Restless Nation* by Ferol Egan and Fremont, *Pathmarker of the West* by Allan Nevins were important sources on the life and times of the "Pathfinder", John C. Fremont, and his western expeditions. *This Reckless Breed of Men* by Robert Glass Cleland, *Across the Wide Missouri* by Bernard deVoto, and *Life in the Far West* by George Ruxton helped me understand the lives of the early mountain men and trappers.

To "hear" the tall-talk voice of the American frontier folk, I turned to *The Tall Tales of Davy Crockett* edited by Michael LoFaro and *Treasury of American Folklore* edited by B.A. Botkin. Life on America's early steamboats is beautifully explained in Mark Twain's *Life on the Mississippi* and in *Steamboating on the Upper Mississippi* by William John Petersen.

For information about the history of astronomy, I am indebted to *Man Discovers the Galaxies* by Berendzen, Hart and Seeley, and *Coming of Age in the Milky Way* by Timothy Ferris. My main source for early American hymns was *Pilgrim Hymnal*, and for nineteenth-century school lessons, I used *Poetical Geography* by George VanWaters, and Peter Parley's *Geography for Children with Nine Maps and Seventy-five Engravings*.

And for information on life in 1840s St Louis, I am grateful to Robert Schnare, Director of the Naval War College Library, for providing me with archival material on early St Louis.

Deep in my bones, I know that somewhere up there, in a place not on any map, my ma rides her white horse. I can almost see her in the starlight . . . leading the ponies down from the hills. Maybe she can help lead us, too – me, Pa, and the dog – lead us on kindly, like a light in the gloom.

I whisper close to his little muskrat head.

—Ready to ride to New Mexico?

And you know what he does, don't you?

He sneezes.

☆ AUTHOR'S NOTE ☆

This story is fiction. Years ago, while researching my book *American Tall Tales*, I read that legendary scout Kit Carson married an Arapaho woman, and together they had a daughter whom he named Adaline. When her mother died, Adaline was sent to live with relatives in St Louis, while her father headed off on explorations with Lieutenant John C. Fremont, known as the "Pathfinder". Hardly anything is known about the real Adaline Carson's life, though one historian quoted a Carson relative as saying Adaline "was a wild girl". Those words haunted me. I sensed that Adaline had been misunderstood and that she had her own story to tell. Soon, a fictional Adaline was born and she provoked this imagined story.

The night I was born on Horse Creek, the sky rained fire. Dogs howled and growled. Arapaho warriors put on red war paint and did a death dance.

Leastwise, that's what Pa tells me. He says my hair was as black as a crow's wing, my eyes the colour of a mud pond; but my skin was the colour of a half-tanned fox hide, plainly showing the mix of white and Indian blood.

My ma told me Pa was so proud he shouted with joy.

—Outta her way and let her ride!

But my Arapaho grandpa, Running-in-a-Circle, did not take an immediate liking to me. He thought I had something to do with the strange doings in the sky.

—The Great Spirit is angry with this birth. He is shooting arrows of fire at us. We must kill her.

—Hold on there, in-law, you're talking wildcat gibberish. She's my little darter.

When things didn't seem to be straightening out, Pa got on his horse and galloped for Bent's Fort. He came back with Doc Hempstead, who wanted to know why there was all this commotion over a tiny half-breed baby.

When Running-in-a-Circle repeated his theory about the fire arrows, Doc set him right.

—Oh, I don't think so. I got me a special knowledge called Science. It explains how a bunch of dirty old rocks sometimes fall through the sky, and when they get near the earth, they burn up. That's the fire you saw. They're called meteors – or falling stars, if you like pretty words. But one thing's certain – they don't have anything to do with the birth of this pretty little mongrel baby.

Running-in-a-Circle sensed that Doc's knowledge had a truth to it and said I could live.

From then on, my white pa called me Adaline.

But my red ma gave me another name: Falling Star.

Eleven years after my fiery birth, I find myself far away from that Arapaho camp on Horse Creek. I'm in St Louis, staying with my cousin Silas, working as a servant in his schoolhouse.

When Pa left me here last spring, he thought I was going to be learning like the others. I figure when he comes back and finds out I was made the official wood hauler and dirt sweeper instead, he's going to smash Cousin Silas to flinders.

—Adaline, are you coming?

From the doorway of the schoolhouse, Cousin Silas snaps his bony fingers.

I clutch my Ma doll closer. I don't ever let go of her, not even when I'm hauling kindling.

—Don't dawdle, girl!

1

I wish I could say, Get your wood yourself, you old apple-headed white man, and put me in the spelling match. I can ring circles around any of your spellers, thanks to Doc Hempstead, who took a liking to me and taught me the alphabet, and Yellow Leaf, my Arapaho grandma, who fed me the eggs of a meadowlark to make me smarter. I'm so good I can spell most anything now. Just ask me – *Constitution? Independence? Rendezvous?* Go on.

But my lips don't move. I never dare talk to that fool. Hold your tongue, darter, was Pa's last words of advice, and ever since, I been as quiet as a rabbit in the grass. Not one word have I spoken to these white folks.

Cousin Silas goes back inside the schoolhouse. As I climb the hill, my back loaded with kindling damp from last night's rain, I clutch my Ma doll tighter and we drift far away. . .

I'm bringing wet wood into Rosalie's kitchen at Bent's Fort in Colorado. Rosalie is half-Mexican and half-French. She cooks for the men at the fort, the fur traders and trappers. She's always singing hymns and right now she sings Look ye, saints, the sight is glorious! *I drop my wood by the fire and my ma takes me on her lap and starts to unbraid my wet hair. Her fingers, so smooth and sure, put me under a happy spell, while Rosalie keeps singing and Doc Hempstead plays his squeaky violin and my pa stands near the door, measuring the wind and rain with some of Doc's shiny new gadgets.*

—Hurry inside, girl, we're freezing!

I carry the load into the classroom, then drop the whole bundle on the hard wooden floor to drown out their lesson. It ain't fair. None of them love spelling like I do.

—Adaline! Work quietly, girl!

I start stacking, fighting the urge to hurl sticks across the room like I hurled them at the wolves the day my ma died.

It's grey and cold. Three wolves stare at me from across the frozen creek. From the distant tepee Running-in-a-Circle beats his tom-tom steadily, trying to strengthen my ma's pulse. She's sick with fever, the same that just killed her ma.

All I can do is throw sticks at the wolves, trying to drive them off. But they don't leave.

Here, in St Louis, Missouri, wolves don't come down from the hills. No sound of the tom-tom tortures my ears.

But it's lonely here. No one talks to me except to order me around. No one knows I can read and write. They think the hair of the black bear's in me because I'm half redskin, and all I'm good for is sweeping floors and fetching wood and water. They never ask me to join in the spelling matches or the guessing games or recite the Lord's Prayer – which I learnt from Doc Hempstead as soon as I could talk – or share the knowledge I've acquired from *Peter Parley's Geography for Children with Nine Maps and Seventy-five Engravings*. Somebody invite me to do just one of these things, and I might break my silence.

I hold on to the thought that when Pa comes to get me after his expedition is over, he's going to roar louder than a grizzly as soon as he hears what Cousin Silas told the whole school on my first day:

—Boys and girls, this is Adaline
mute, and none too smart, and I'm s
she has the devilish mixture of white and
blood. She's going to be working for us, so I a
you to kindly show her your Christian love. But
always keep an eye out for her, because she is and
always will be part savage.

When is Pa coming back for me?

That's the question I ask a hundred times a day, and I'm asking it again right now as I trail home from the schoolhouse behind Lilly and the Ruxton brothers.

I clutch my Ma doll, the dolly Pa gave me five months ago when he left me with Cousin Silas.

It was our first day in St Louis, and I'd seen a string of wonders – stone roads, huge boats with chimney stacks blowing black clouds, girls calling, "Hot corn! Hot corn!", hundreds of brick houses and stores, and thousands of people.

The most people I'd ever seen before that was at the Green River Rendezvous, when all the trappers and Indians used to get together in August, the time the beavers were moulting their pelts and couldn't be trapped for hats. That was the time for mountain men like Pa to drink and play cards, trade guns and buffalo hides, and brag their fool heads off.

But there was never more than a few hundred folks at the Rendezvous. Here in St Louis, the carriage driver told me and Pa there was twenty-five thousand. How did he know that? Did he stand on a corner and count them all?

Just as we pulled up to Cousin Silas's redbrick house, Pa pulled something out of his bag. It looked like a bunch of green corn husks.

—Here's a dolly I made for you, darter, in case you get lonesome while I'm gone.

The doll had no face, nor even a patch of cornsilk for hair. Pa had just tied strings around the husks to make a neck and a waist.

I took it with a scowl. Couldn't he see I was too old to play with dollies?

—Be polite now. Don't go poking your nose everywhere like a dog. And most of all – hold your tongue till I get back. Can you do that, darter?

I narrowed my eyes at him. He knows I like to say what I please.

—I mean it, Adaline. Folks might not understand your grit.

I nodded grudgingly. No sassy talking.

—And learn good.

Before he opened the carriage door, I tugged on the collar of his buckskin shirt and pulled him close. I breathed in the dusty smell of his leather jacket and pipe tobacco, then growled in his ear.

—When you comin' back for me?

—I tole you a hundred times, I don't know exactly. Sometime before winter.

I gripped him harder, pulled him closer, and talked meaner.

—I'm still wishin' to go with you.

—I know you are. But you can't.

I looked at Cousin Silas's redbrick house, at the white painted porch and flower bushes. The front door opened and out came Pa's cousins: skinny, dried up-looking Silas, plump-cheeked Opal, and little red-haired, pouty-mouthed Lilly.

I turned quickly back to Pa.

—You won't forget me, will you?

—Forget you? 'Course not.

—You won't stop loving me?

He looked at me, almost fierce. He pressed his rough finger against my nose.

—I'll always love you, darter, like an old squirrel loves a nut.

Then he coughed and stepped out of the carriage to greet his kin.

Lilly and Opal stood back while Cousin Silas shook Pa's hand.

—We're mighty pleased to see you, Kit. Can you stay a while to visit?

—No, sir. I'm late three days joining the Fremont expedition already. Gotta catch the boat this afternoon. Come on out, Adaline!

When I didn't come out of the carriage, Pa opened the door and yanked me out.

—This here's Adaline, my little darter.

Pa's kin stared at me like I was a two-headed dog. I knew right then he'd neglected to tell them I was a half-breed.

But Pa didn't see their faces because he was grinning at me.

—My Adaline's a spunky child. Doc Hempstead at the fort says she's extremely bright. It's a fact, my darter's got more 'n enough—

Silas interrupted in a low, sad tone.

—Oh, you don't have to apologize for her, Kit. We understand.

—I wasn't apologizing, Silas.

An awkward silence followed. Cousin Opal and Lilly looked like they were about to vomit.

I was wishing Pa would finish telling them what he'd started, the words he sometimes said to me – Darter, you got more 'n enough brains to be the president of these United States!

It was a dreadful pity he didn't say that to the folks who needed to hear it most. But it was a heap more dreadful he didn't mention he intended for me to go to their school.

Cousin Silas broke the silence.

—Don't worry, we can handle trouble, cousin – with the Lord's help.

Pa frowned and looked at me a moment, like he

wasn't sure any more about leaving me with his kin.

I frowned back at him, showing I agreed one hundred per cent with his doubts.

But then he just sighed, like he couldn't see a way out.

—OK, darter. You're in the land of apples and book-larnin' now. Make the most of it.

Pa turned back to the carriage. I let out a cry and leaped for him like I was leaping for my life. Pa took me by the shoulders. Then he leaned over and stared me in the eye. A painful look crossed his face. He spoke soft so nobody else could hear.

—You give me your word you'll wait for me, Adaline? Come better or worse?

His fierce, sad eyes made me nod *yes*.

—Good. Then I give you my word I'll be back for you.

Without a goodbye to anybody, he climbed up with the driver. Then the carriage took off and I was left stiff with sorrow, wishing I didn't have another minute to live.

The truth is, no sorrow of mine could have

stopped Pa from going. It was written in the Book of Fate that he was to be the official guide on a special mission for Lieutenant John C. Fremont of the Army Corps of Engineers, who folks call the Pathfinder. Pa was going to help the Pathfinder lead an expedition through the Rocky Mountains.

When I turned around and saw my cousins staring at me, I felt like I was looking at a bag of vipers and copperheads. I can say now I was not far wrong.

Cousin Silas looked mad and disgusted.

—Why didn't he warn us you were half-Injun? That he'd gone and got himself mixed up with a squaw woman?

Then and there I decided not to talk to them folks, not just sassy talk, but *all* talk. Once I opened my mouth I'd be a goner.

—What's wrong with you, girl? Are you a mute?

I nodded.

—Oh, my stars, Silas! What's your cousin done now? What's he expect us to do with her?

—Put her to work, I reckon.

Of course, at that moment I should have screamed *No!* and shot off down the street. But I was shackled by my promise to Pa. I'd given him my word I'd wait for him, come better or worse.

When we got inside their big, fancy house, Opal put me in a little room off the kitchen. She ordered me to put on some of Lilly's cast-offs – an iron corset, an ugly pink dress, and a pair of leather shoes so stiff you'd have to chew them for a week to soften them. And she ordered her slave Caddie to burn my buckskin leggings and shirt and moccasins as soon as I took them all off.

Alone in my room, I pulled off my things and was staring at the corset not knowing what to do with it when Caddie came in and reached for my clothes.

I snatched them away from her and gave her a look that said I'd kill her if she tried to touch them again.

My meanness didn't seem to scare her. Her eyes looked sorrowful as she studied my bare body.

—Lord, what happened to you, child? Looks like somebody worked you over with an axe.

I just glared at her. The fact was, I'd done it to myself three months earlier when my ma had died. I'd butchered off my braids with a hunting knife, then slashed my limbs, cutting my own flesh. My scars still looked raw, and my hair had grown back only a few centimetres.

—You're sure a pitiful sight.

She reached out to touch me and I growled at her.

She backed off and looked at me sad-like.

—I ain't going to hurt you, child. Looks like you been hurt enough. Go ahead and get dressed now. I'll fix you something to eat.

She left, and I shoved my buckskins under the bed.

Later I ate by myself in a corner of the kitchen, and all that same night I lay awake, clutching the corn-husk dolly Pa gave me, trying to figure how I was going to live without him or my ma. In the darkest hour, I started saying the hymn Rosalie used to sing when she missed her kin:

*Lead, kindly light, amid the encircling gloom;
lead me on; the night is dark, and I am far
from home.*

I was saying the hymn over and over when a
miracle occurred: the dolly Pa gave me started
talking. Not out-loud words, but quiet ones,
invisible ones you could only hear with your heart.

—*Don't cry, Falling Star. I am with you.
Remember the story of Little Skunk? One day he
got lost. But his ma looked far and wide until she
found him, cold and shivering in a dark cave.*

I could smell Ma's sweet scent of sage and
smoked grass.

—*Sleep, my child, and I will hold your little fur
face and your little fur feet and you will always be
safe with me.*

The corn-husk dolly was holding my ma's spirit!
I was sure of it.

Her words gave me a peaceful feeling. A calm
came over me, and I went to sleep like a baby
wrapped in the down of cat-tail rushes.

My Ma doll's been talking to me ever since. It makes me feel the way another one of Rosalie's hymns says: *Alone and yet not alone, am I.*

—She carries it everywhere, even to prayer time in the parlour.

Lilly's telling the Ruxton brothers about my Ma doll, making me sound like a crazy person.

The Ruxtons are new to the school, and Lilly's already made friends with them. She's real nice to the other children, too, but she treats me like I'm covered with fleas.

Now they all twist their necks to get a good look at me and my doll, then turn away, giggling like girls.

—She holds it close to her ear sometimes, like this . . . like she's waiting for it to talk.

Lilly shows them how I hold my doll.

—Whatever you do, don't touch it.

The hair on the back of my neck starts to go up.

—Why? What'll she do?

—You don't want to know.

—What'll she do? Tell us, tell us!

She leans in to them, her eyes fixed on me, and whispers just loud enough for me to hear.

—She'll scalp you!

The boys scream and laugh.

My heart starts to pound, because one of the Ruxtons gets a look in his eye.

—Let's see what she does.

He dances a bit towards me.

—Leave her alone, Robert!

—I ain't scared. Hey, Injun!

He dances closer.

I fix my most evil glare on him. Ain't nobody tried to touch my Ma doll before.

He dances closer and closer.

—Robert, don't make her mad! Don't touch that stinky devil doll!

Stinky devil doll. You want to see the devil? Lie low and watch.

I let out a bloodcurdling whoop – the most crazy, hateful sound you've ever heard come from a human skull – and start running after them.

They jump straight up in the air, like they've

been shot. Then they all tear down the road, hollering.

Robert cries out for mercy. But it's Lilly I'm after.

She seems about to die with screaming and fright, holding on to her curly red hair, like she thinks I'm going to rip it out with my bare hands.

I stop running and watch them all fly off like screeching blue jays.

I clutch my Ma doll while my heart slows down. It ain't worth it – wasting my strength on the likes of them.

Every day, as soon as I get back from working at the school, I have to go to work in the kitchen. Right now I'm pitting cherries as Caddie rolls out dough for a pie.

Voices waft out from the parlour:

—She's crazy, Mama. When Robert Ruxton tried to touch her stinky doll, she screamed like a demon and ran after us.

—Lilly.

—I mean it, Mama. She's a lunatic. You should have seen the look in her eyes. She meant to scalp me.

Lilly starts to cry, and then I don't hear any more. Cousin Opal must have shut the door.

Caddie glances at me, trying to hide a little smile. But then she shakes her head and gives a warning.

—Don't tease Miss Lilly, child. She can be mighty vengeful.

That little mosquiter? I'd like her to see the results of true scalping like the first time I did: see the Cheyenne dance in the moonlight after a fight, waving the bloody scalps of Pawnees on the ends of their willow wands. Like to see her vomit for two days after, like I did. Third or fourth time, she'd get used to it.

The more I pit the cherries, the sadder I start to get. Truth is, every minute I spend in this house is a terrible waste of my time, time I could be spending with Pa and John C. Fremont, the Pathfinder.

The Pathfinder's leading twenty-eight men and teams of mules and horses over the plains. They're mapping a path through the Wind River Mountains of the Rockies, and they're scientifically naming all the plants and rocks and winged and crawly things they see along the way. When Pa told me a twelve-year-old boy, the Pathfinder's brother-in-law, would be travelling with them, I went wild.

—I should be going! Not him! I'm the one part Indian! I got the blood that knows the trail better 'n that chicken-livered, pale-faced boy! I should be the one to go!

—Likely you should be, darter. But he happens to be two things you're not.

—What?

—Kin to John Fremont, and more important, a feller.

His words don't cut my wrath. Not one bit.

—It ain't fair to be a girl when you ain't even pretty.

—You're somethin' better 'n pretty, Adaline.

—What am I? What?

—I can't tell you what you are. You're the one who's got to find that out.

The Pathfinder.

That's what I'm aching to be.

That name quickens my heart, makes me want to tear my hair out, what I got left. I'm dying to march with the Pathfinder, breathe in the dust of the buffalo runs, make willow mats to bridge creeks,

21

hear the mule teamsters howl *Gee!* and *Haw!*

Now my heart beats like it's filled with bird wings. I ache to tear out the back door into the twilight and soar into the unknown.

All at once I'm exhausted from my yearning. I can't go nowhere. I don't know where I'd go. Plus I gave Pa my word.

The cherry juice makes my hands look like they're covered with blood. Caddie hands me a rag. I wipe my hands and rest on a stool.

—*Ma, what am I?*

—*You cannot answer that question inside a house that does not love you, Falling Star. Ask your question to the fresh morning air.*

Her answer calms me. I remember how we rode together mornings when I was small, leading the ponies down from the hills. I sat in front of her on her white horse, clinging to its mane. Her long braids fell over my shoulders as if they were mine.

—*Is there early morning, Ma, in the Land-Behind-the-Stars?*

—*A dream of morning. A wisp of pink, trailing through the heart.*

When I turn around, I catch Caddie giving me a sideways look. I reckon I might have been whispering aloud. I reckon she might know now I can talk.

She turns to face me full front. Our eyes lock a moment, and she smiles a blossom smile, beautiful as a moonflower opening in the night.

She touches her finger to her lips.

—Keep your secrets, child, keep them all to yourself.

Alone in my room, I'm reaching into my bag of possibles, the bag that holds all my personal property.

First I take out the book Doc Hempstead gave me from his library: *The Heavenly Bodies* by Professor William van der Waters.

—*Young lady, if you're a falling star, you should learn more about yourself.*

Next I take out the eagle feather and carved dragonfly my ma gave me before she died.

—*With the eagle feather, soar to great heights, Falling Star. With the dragonfly, move through a battle without being harmed.*

Then I pull out the tinderbox Pa gave me on our trip here when we were camped under a half-moon.

—*Keep your firelight low, darter, and in the*

mornin' always erase all your signs and tracks.

Pa and I kept our light low for fifty nights, travelling overland with the St Vrain caravan from Bent's Fort in Colorado to St Louis, Missouri. We travelled along the north bank of the Arkansas and the River of Lost Souls and Big Salt Bottom and Walnut Creek and on to Independence, Missouri.

Pa promised me a different kind of adventure for our trip back. After he comes to get me, we'll board a steamboat on the Mississippi River, then catch the waters of the Missouri and steam all the way to Kansas Landing. A steamboat! I ain't ever been on one before. Travelling with Pa on a steamer seems the next best thing to travelling with the Pathfinder.

There's a tap on my door.

—Adaline?

It's Cousin Opal.

—Come to the parlour now.

Evening prayer time. I slip Pa's tinderbox into my pocket and carry my Ma doll tight under my arm.

When I enter the cold parlour, Lilly scurries to

the corner, as far away from me as she can get.

Opal scowls at her daughter, then looks back at me and smiles. Her false smile makes me more wary than Lilly's silly fear. Opal's dying to make me different than I am.

I go and sit stiffly in one of the mean, straight chairs. Silas pulls his spectacles down on his skinny nose, opens his Bible, and starts reciting:

—"When thou prayest, enter into thy closet, and when thou has shut the door, pray to thy Father which is in secret. . . "

—*Dear Pa, come get me, take me from these hateful folks, I beseech thee.*

Silas drones on, draining all the life and joy and blood out of Scripture. I try to take flight. I clutch my tinderbox and hug my doll tight. With my eyes squeezed shut and my mind concentrated, my box and my corn husks shift into the shapes of the two people I've loved most in the world:

A young Arapaho woman stands by a tree near a stream in the morning mist. She's breaking off branches for her family's fire.

A handsome trapper is chasing wild horses near

Bent's Fort. It's early fall, the Time-of-the-Plum-Moon, and the Arapaho are camped on Horse Creek, under the cottonwoods.

When the trapper sees the girl, he's nearly knocked off his horse by her beauty. Her long hair shines blue-black in the early morning light, and her cheeks are bright as berries. She wears a buckskin dress and leggings and delicate beaded moccasins and shiny little earbobs.

The trapper don't know Arapaho very well, but he's a good sign talker. Using his hands, he makes the inquiry:

—What are you? A human girl? Or a beautiful bird?

—A beautiful bird, she signs back.

Later, the trapper learns she's the daughter of the band's medicine man, Running-in-a-Circle, and his wife, Yellow Leaf. And one night, he ties his best horse to her pa's tepee. The next day, when the trapper sees his horse has been added to the Arapaho band, he knows the beautiful bird can be his wife.

Her people called her Singing Wind. My pa

called her Alice. I called her Ma. And when we lived at Bent's Fort, the trappers called her Kit Carson's squaw.

It was last March when she died, the Time-of-the-Light-Snow-Moon. Pa was trapping in the Rockies while Ma and I stayed on Horse Creek. When the fever swept through, it got Yellow Leaf first, then Ma.

Running-in-a-Circle thought his people were being pierced by the Pawnees' invisible poison arrows. All day and night he held my ma's wrist and beat his drum in time to her pulse, trying to make it stronger.

I thumped my own hand against my heart to send her the message that I could not live without her.

But she left anyway and followed her ma on the trail of ghosts leading to the Land-Behind-the-Stars.

After she left I tore my clothes and chopped off my braids to show my grief the way the Arapaho do when someone they love dies. I slashed my arms and legs with a knife until my blood streamed over my moccasins.

When Pa showed up, he went wild. He blamed

Running-in-a-Circle for my ma's death and he was furious that I had cut myself up. He rushed me to Doc Hempstead at the fort, before I could follow Ma on the ghost trail. Then he left me with Doc and Rosalie and disappeared into the Rockies for weeks. When Pa returned, he looked near death himself, wasted from his grief. I reckon we both tried different ways to go after my ma, but in the end, we both knew we had to stay here a while longer.

Pa wouldn't talk about my ma after that, not one single word, and he wouldn't let me visit Horse Creek again, either. I was aching to go there when I heard Running-in-a-Circle had got sick himself. But I didn't talk to Pa about it. I was afraid he'd get all stirred up again and leave.

I never blamed Running-in-a-Circle for my ma's death. I imagine that in her fever, when she saw her ma starting out on the shiny path of the ghost trail, she dropped everything and ran after her, forgetting all she was leaving behind.

But now she seems to be remembering. Though she lives in the Land-Behind-the-Stars, her spirit has found me. At this moment, I hear her whisper a song that mixes the religion of her people with the religion of Pa's:

Praise ye, Great Holy Spirit, sun and moon.
Praise ye, and all ye stars of light. . .

Her song puts me in the twilight outside Running-in-a-Circle's tepee.

I smell the green trees, the green grass and the blue smoke of the Arapaho fire. I dance with my ma around the flame.

—Adaline, prayer time is over.

I see Running-in-a-Circle offer his pipe to the sky.

—She's under the devil's spell, Papa.

Thank ye, Great Spirit, for the moon—

—Open your eyes, girl! Right now!

And for the stars, O Holy Spirit, amen.

My book on the Heavenly Bodies is right hard to understand, but I've been trying to read it for months now. I'm anxious to acquire the knowledge of Science, knowledge like my pa and the Pathfinder have.

> During the early 1700s, powerful new telescopes allowed scientists to better understand the map of the heavens. Were they seeing the entire universe? Or were there, in fact, other galaxies beyond ours?

I stare at the book, as quiet as a creek on a hot day, and ponder *map of the heavens, entire universe, other galaxies.*

I'd like to roll these words around in my hand like smooth stones or chew on them like pieces of buffalo skin.

I clutch my Ma doll tight.

—*Ma, I dreadful want the knowledge of Science. I want to map the heavens, like Pa and the Pathfinder map the earth.*

—*Beware, Falling Star.*

Why does she say that? Before I can ask, I hear voices in the kitchen, on the other side of my door.

—I'm scared of her, Mama. What if she plans to murder us all in our sleep like that adopted Mohawk boy who cut the family on the river? Knifed them all in their beds and set the house on fire!

They must not know I can hear them. They must think I'm working down in the garden with Caddie.

—Hush. You must soften your heart towards Adaline, Lilly. If we show her love and kindness, we can wash away the Indian stain.

Vipers and copperheads. Only not so honest. These serpents don't have wide-open jaws and long fangs. Instead, they got poison words. If I was a flash of lightning, I'd strike them both.

—But when is Cousin Kit coming back for her, Mama? When?

—I told you, Lilly, when his expedition is over.

—But I heard Papa tell you the expedition is *already* over. Papa said he was afraid Cousin Kit was never coming back for her.

—You shouldn't listen to our—

—But what if he *never* comes for her, Mama? What then?

Her voice fades, and I don't hear Opal's answer. They must have left the kitchen.

I feel cold all over, so cold my teeth crack against one another.

What's she mean, Pa's expedition is over? What's she mean, Cousin Silas is afraid Pa's not coming back for me?

I ain't never thought of such a thing. It's not possible. He gave me his word.

I squeeze my Ma doll.

—*Ma, what's Lilly talking about?*

—*Be still, Falling Star. Remember the story of*

Little Frog. . . One day an evil snake moved slyly along the bank of the river. Little Frog's ma whispered, Keep still, my child, or the snake will see you and eat you. Do not hop away until he has gone to sleep.

I'm helping Caddie peel potatoes.

There's no way Pa ain't coming back for me. I ain't worried. Fact is, my pa would do anything for me – he'd fight grizzlies for me, he'd wrestle rattlesnakes and mountain cats. If I was hungry, he'd give me his last bite. If I was lame, he'd carry me a hundred miles.

The only thing might keep him a little longer is if he had to help a friend, like the time he was days late coming to the fort because he was rescuing a trapper kidnapped by Utes.

A mission like that could be keeping him now. But you can be sure when he's all done, he'll come straight for me, faster than lightning buttered with quicksilver.

In the next room, Lilly starts up her lessons with

Cousin Opal. Caddie keeps her back to the noise, but I stop peeling to hear Lilly read aloud:

"Two continents only, on this globe are seen –
Eastern and Western, are their names I ween;
The Eastern continent, we see, divide,
In Europe, Africa and Asia wide."

I'm holding my breath, a durn thief, aching to steal her book learning. I'm a mix, I reckon, of white and red blood, and also a jumbled love for free roaming and the Fruits of Civilization, which is what Doc Hempstead calls reading, writing and geography.

Lilly starts reading something else to Opal:

—"The people of Asia are more en-en –"

—Enlightened.

—"Enlightened than the people of Africa. The people of darkest Africa still live like animals. They are cruel and fer-fer –"

—Ferocious.

—Ferocious. But what about Caddie, Mama? She's from darkest Africa. She's not ferocious.

—That's because her spirit's been tamed, darling. She's been baptized and converted from her heathen ways.

Vipers and copperheads.

I glance at Caddie, but she don't look at me.

I yearn to touch her cheek. She's beautiful, with her dark skin in the yellow glaze of the firelight. I'd be proud if she would let me read to her.

But she's cautioned me to keep silent. We're both in a strange land and must hold our secrets close.

Cousin Silas comes bursting into the kitchen carrying a letter. He's breathing hard and smiling. He moves past me and Caddie like we're invisible.

In the parlour, he talks excitedly to Cousin Opal.

—Captain Peterson has accepted our invitation for dinner on Tuesday.

—Lovely, dear. We'll dine on the lawn, weather permitting. We can set the table on the grass, under the oak. Adaline can help Caddie serve.

—No, Mama! Not Adaline. She'll scare everybody off!

—Oh, don't be silly. I'll dress her in one of your party dresses.

—No, Mama! It'll stink!

—An old one, precious, don't worry. One you never wear any more.

—I don't know, Opal. . .

—Pshaw, Silas. Adaline will be fine. She obeys Caddie. She's scared of her.

—No doubt. All Injuns are scared of Negroes.

Caddie and I don't even look at each other. Some things you just got to pretend you don't hear. They're too evil.

I'm trying to be patient and not worry about Pa's coming for me. If I start to yearn too much, I'll jump out of my skin.

So I'm forcing myself to read *The Heavenly Bodies* by candlelight:

> In 1750, an English astronomer theorized that millions of stars made up the Milky Way. He said there were millions more star systems like it.

Millions like it – how can that be? If there are

millions and millions, then where is the Land-Behind-the-Stars? I'd been picturing it right up there behind the first ten stars of night, with my ma and Yellow Leaf living there.

> In 1781, William Herschel deter-mined that it would take six hundred years to examine the entire night sky with a telescope.

I slam the book shut and spit this knowledge out. Don't want it. It banishes the Arapaho land to a place beyond the beyond – too far away for any dead Indian to find.

With a shiver, I blow out my candle and squeeze my Ma doll.

When I close my eyes, one of Rosalie's songs comes to me in the dark:

> *Watchman, tell us of the night,*
> *What its signs of promise are.*

I'm sitting under a tree outside the school eating my bread.

The children are playing a game, holding a long rope and weaving over the grass like a snake. They're laughing and squealing and now all falling down.

I don't know how much longer I can wait for my pa. Even though I gave my word, I've a mind to rise from the grass this minute and head back to Colorado on my own. It ain't but a couple of miles from here to the Mississippi. I know the Mississippi River would take me to the Missouri River. And I know the Missouri River would take me all the way to Kansas Landing where I could hook up with a fur caravan going back to Bent's Fort.

Once I got there, I could stay with Rosalie till Pa showed up. He'll be madder than a hornet because I didn't wait for him. But I'll shoot my fist through the air and shout, Serves you right for not coming for me the second you was free!

Of course, it would worry him something fierce if he was to show up here in St Louis to get me and find out I'd already taken off on my own.

I look back at Lilly and the other children playing. My plan evaporates. I can't run away now; I can't break my word to Pa.

The snake collapses with screams of laughter. As everyone scrambles back up, Lilly sneaks a glance my way. There's a look of pity in her eyes, like she's been working on softening her heart towards me.

She separates from the others and comes over to where I'm sitting.

I clutch my Ma doll tight and study my bread like I ain't never seen bread before.

—Adaline?

I don't look up.

—It makes me sad seeing you sitting here all by yourself.

I glance at her as she sits near me on the grass. She does look right sad, actually. And it puts me off my guard.

She sighs real deep, then her voice quavers like she's touched by what she's about to say.

—I'm sorry I've been mean all the months you've been here. I know now that you can't help it.

What's she mean?

—Your birth wasn't your doing. I know that. But you must have done some sinning before you were born, or you wouldn't have been born half red.

I look down at the grass.

—Otherwise, it just wouldn't be fair, and our God in heaven is all-fair and all-loving.

This conversation is taking a strange turn.

—I was thinking, if you started asking for forgiveness night and day, maybe you'd grow different.

I clutch my Ma doll so tight, the corn husks crack.

—Maybe the white part of you would grow over the red part. Think of it. The heathen part would dry up. You'd learn to talk and your hair would start to curl. And I could have you for my sister. Would you like that?

I glance at her. Her bow mouth smiles at me like I'm made of candy.

—My heart would be made glad, Adaline, if you was to get forgiveness and be like us.

My eyes narrow into slits. I can't help it. The thought of being like her makes me feel mean.

She pulls back, scared-like.

—Adaline?

I keep my eyes narrow and my lip starts to curl.

She gasps, then starts to snivel.

—Adaline, please don't ever scalp me. Please don't hurt my mama or papa.

Oh, I see. The little coward almost had me fooled about wanting me to be her sister and all. Her fear of me is so pitiful I can't help but try and make it worse. I show my teeth, then snap at her like a wolf.

She squeals and scrambles to her feet.

I laugh, but I'm afraid Lilly has no sense of fun. She goes from tears to a kind of breathless anger.

—It-it-it won't help for you to ask God for forgiveness, Adaline. You'll always be a savage! You'll be wicked and ferocious your whole life! And God will smite you, Adaline!

Before I can bite the air again, she runs off to join the screaming snake of children weaving over the grass.

Lilly's old corset is hugging me tighter 'n a bear, and her old party shoes are biting my toes worse 'n the meanest fish in the creek. I'm crippled and breathless helping Caddie clear the table under the walnut tree, while Cousin Silas, Captain Peterson and Reverend Wallace smoke cigars and drink brandy.

The captain is talking.

—Heard a good one yesterday. Seems General Clark once entertained some Washington visitors by inviting a bunch of redskins over. The savages put on their full regalia and did a war dance. Afterwards, this French doctor got the idea to lay booby traps with electric batteries all around the house. And whenever a curious Injun touched one, he jumped like a rabbit and went screaming away!

Silas and the reverend laugh.

—But let me tell you, that doctor was known for giving the Injuns *free* vaccinations – no charge, none whatsoever. A right decent man.

I glare at the talker puffing on his cigar.

What I'd like to say to him is this: the Indians do not have the knowledge of Science. But when a white man visits an Arapaho tepee no one plays tricks on him. The old women drag out buffalo hides and invite him to sit. The girls serve him dried cherries mixed with buffalo marrow. And in the rosy haze of the firelight, the men share their pipe.

The captain looks over at me.

—What's your girl staring at, Silas?

—Oh, don't worry about her. She won't do any harm. She's got corn pone for brains. Go on, Adaline, do your work.

They all laugh – but nervously – because I keep my eyes fixed on them.

—She's the daughter of your cousin, Kit Carson. Isn't that right, Silas?

—That's right. I'm afraid he went native on us.

Didn't tell us she was an Injun when he wrote asking us to look after her while he went on the Fremont expedition. Didn't even tell us she was a mute.

—A mute?

—Yep, seems to hear OK. She can holler, too. Just can't talk.

—Well, your burden might be coming to an end, Silas. I hear the expedition is over. It was quite a success, I understand.

—I heard that myself a couple of weeks ago, Captain. But where in tarnation is my cousin?

—Can't say. But the fact is, Fremont and some of his men are on their way to St Louis right now to meet with the governor.

My heart starts to pound.

—Fremont's coming here?

—It's what I heard.

The Pathfinder's coming here? What about my pa? My pa?

—Well, when are they coming, Captain? Have you heard that?

—Seems they'll be here on Friday – when the

47

steamboat comes down from Kansas Landing.

Friday? Friday? I can't breathe!

—Do you know, Captain, if Kit Carson is travelling with the party?

—Don't know for sure, but I suspect he might be. Make a good show for the governor.

My pa's coming!

I look at Caddie. She smiles her moonflower smile and whispers to me.

—He's comin', child. Your pappy's coming to save you.

I knew it! I knew it! It's a good thing I waited! If I was wearing a hat I'd fling it high into the air. If I had me a bell, I'd ring it till their ears fell off.

Praise ye, Heavenly Father! Praise ye, Great Holy Spirit! Praise ye, Ma doll! Praise ye *all* for fixing things right!

I dance on the grass like a goat in the dusky light, whooping my triumph – till Cousin Silas catches hold of my apron and snaps me to stillness.

—Stop that hollerin', girl! You're scaring my guests!

I throw back my head and walk puffed up with airs towards the house. The Pathfinder's coming! And my pa's coming with him! Can't none of them touch me now.

Outta my way and let me ride.

As light creeps into my room, Caddie pokes her head in the doorway.

—Child?

I'm lying in my bed. I haven't slept a wink. I can't stop smiling, can't stop dreaming or trembling with happiness.

—I brought you a dress to wear for your pa.

I frown. I don't know about that. My pa likes me in buckskins. A dress won't do.

But Caddie goes on talking like she's reading my mind.

—Don't worry. This one's pretty – not like them ugly cast-offs of Miss Lilly's.

I sit up. Well, I might like something pretty to wear. I might.

—It's blue.

Caddie holds out a little blue dress.

It *is* pretty. I nod and she comes over.

—Hold up your arms.

I hold them up. And she slides the sleeves of the dress down them and takes the neck over my head.

—Get up.

I jump up and stand by the bed and she brushes the dress down around my knees.

—Turn 'round.

I turn around and she buttons a long string of buttons up the back. You can hear the both of us breathing softly.

—Uh-huh. Pretty, real pretty. Let's see 'bout that hair now.

She pats down my hair. Her hands feel soft and smooth like my ma's. My head curls down like a kitten's.

—Let me see.

I let her see.

She takes my face in her hands and shakes her head.

—You need a bonnet.

A bonnet? I don't know. I'm not the type to

wear a bonnet. Pa won't recognize me in a bonnet.

—Hold still.

She pulls a blue bonnet out of her apron pocket and puts it on me and ties a big bow under my chin.

—There. Real pretty. I'll tell Miss Opal I made this for you.

Her eyes fill with tears.

I look at her curious-like.

She sighs.

—Truth is, I had me a little girl of my own one time. I made this dress and bonnet for her.

She turns to go.

I grab her hands and look in her eyes, asking with mine, *What happened to your daughter?*

But she pulls away and covers her face and gives out one long sob.

I try to hug her, but she gently pulls away and starts to leave the room.

I grab her skirt, trying to get her to look at me.

But she won't.

She slips off without another word.

☆ ☆ ☆

If you were riding through the streets of St Louis in a fine carriage on a bright, sunny morning, and you were wearing a pretty blue dress and a pretty blue bonnet, and you were fixing to meet up with Lieutenant John C. Fremont and Mr Kit Carson, nobody would be apt to point at you and say, Phew, what an ugly Injun.

They might even say, Hey, look at that pretty girl ridin' in that carriage.

And you'd ride on by them and wave at them – white people, black people, red people, brown people, priests, soldiers; women in caps and petticoats dragging dirty children along behind them; men with handkerchiefs tied around their heads, pulling carts of wood; whole families pulling their wagons loaded with furniture, pigs and chickens – all of them headed for the Mississippi.

And when you arrived at the shining shore, you'd see rivermen with long poles pushing flatboats and steamboat men loading up their freight. You'd see clouds of black smoke, whirls of fiery cinders and giant paddle wheels churning the water, and you'd hear the bells and the whistles and the splashing, and you'd feel your heart pounding so hard you'd have to press your Ma doll against your chest to keep from exploding.

My heart tells her now that I can't live another minute without seeing my pa. And to my heart, she whispers back.

—*Be calm, Falling Star. You are my dear, beautiful daughter.*

I like to hear that. I do feel a bit beautiful in Caddie's daughter's blue dress and bonnet. I expect to knock Pa off his perch when he sees me. And I don't think I will tell him I was made a servant at the school. And I won't rip his ears off if he confesses he lingered a week or two longer than he really had to. Bygones can be bygones.

I picture him putting his hand in mine, then taking me back to Silas's house, only long enough to have supper and get my things. Pa will tip his hat and say, Thankee, folks, but I hope you don't mind if me and my darter don't stay the night. We have to get on the river as soon as possible so we can catch up with the St Vrain caravan that's leaving Kansas Landing in a few weeks.

I'll linger only long enough to hug Caddie good-bye and give her the eagle feather Ma gave me so she can soar to great heights. I'll leave her my carved dragonfly, too, so she can dart through a battle without being harmed.

I won't need these things any more, because I'll have my pa.

And the two of us will take off down the road to the Mississippi. And after our steamboat travels to Kansas Landing, we'll hook up with the fur caravan and I'll ride in the cook wagon and Pa will set off each morning to get our food.

At twilight he'll return with buffalo meat. And when it's singing in the pot, I'll pull a blanket around me and listen to his yarns about the

Pathfinder's expedition: the wildfire he saw, the white wolf, the human remains. Or worse things – a big grizzly, a monster snake, a scalping Blackfoot! What gives most folks the trembles only fires up Pa.

I'm just like him. I'm all fired up now, standing on the riverbank with Cousin Silas and Cousin Opal, waiting to catch sight of Pa's sandy hair, his leather coat with the silver buttons. It won't be long now. A boat's unloading, and there's a big commotion around it, like some important persons are about to get off. Folks are twisting their necks and peering over each others' heads like any second these special ones are going to step forward.

My heart's thumping out of my chest. I can't wait to see my pa – or the Pathfinder. I have a feeling by now Pa's convinced the Pathfinder I can outrun, outride, outwalk any traveller on the trail. Next expedition, I'll be with them for sure.

Cousin Silas sucks in his breath.

—Lookee there.

He squints against the sun and points at a man with black curly hair, a black beard, and a blue uniform with gold braid, standing as straight as a chief.

—Is that Fremont, Silas?

—I reckon it is.

The Pathfinder! I can't wait. Clutching my Ma doll, I break into a dogtrot.

—Adaline!

But I keep going, tearing through the crowd now like a Kansas tornado.

I can't see Pa yet. He must be coming up behind the Pathfinder.

More folks step off the boat. I look for Pa's sunny face, his sandy hair, but I still don't see him. I keep pushing past folks till I get right down to the landing. I start to climb aboard the boat, but a man in a bandanna pushes me back.

—Get outta here, you redskin rascal! There's nothing on this boat for you.

I stop, surprised he could see the real me under my pretty bonnet. Cousin Silas grabs my arm.

—Adaline! Get back here!

He pulls me away from the boat and shouts to John C. Fremont.

—Lieutenant Fremont, may I have a word with you?

The Pathfinder is talking to some men who are writing down everything he says.

Cousin Silas shouts at him again.

—Sir! Sir! Is Mr Christopher Carson with you?

John C. Fremont glances at Cousin Silas and shakes his head.

—Can you tell me where he is? I'm his cousin. Silas Carson.

John C. Fremont gives Silas a serious look-over and nods hello.

—Pleased to meet you. Your cousin Kit's headed off to New Mexico.

—New Mexico?

New Mexico?

—How long's he planning to stay there?

—For ever, he reckons. *I* reckon it's just till I need a good scout again.

For ever? What's he mean?

—But how can that be, sir? What about his daughter here?

—What daughter?

Silas pushes me forward.

—This girl here is Kit Carson's daughter, Miss Adaline Carson.

The Pathfinder looks at me like he's looking at a skinned rabbit.

—Carson never mentioned a daughter to me.

—Surely he did.

—Certainly not.

—He never told you about his Injun wife and half-breed daughter?

John C. Fremont looks Silas up and down.

—Not a word, sir. Could it be that you are accusing him of your own mistake?

—I beg your pardon?

—Could you be trying to pass off your own half-breed as the daughter of Kit Carson?

—What?

—Don't try to hoodwink me, my friend. Or I'll have you arrested.

The Pathfinder then turns away, dismissing us

like we're a couple of frauds, and he sets to answering more questions.

Cousin Silas got stung bad. He yanks me back from the crowd and angrily moves me towards the carriage where Cousin Opal is waiting.

I haven't fully grasped the notion that Pa's not here. I crane my neck and try to see over my shoulder, see if maybe he's about to step off the boat. Maybe that man wasn't really the Pathfinder. I know the Pathfinder ain't mean like that man.

—Move, girl! He's not coming back for you. He played us both for fools!

Cousin Silas gives me a shove towards the carriage.

He starts to push me again and that's when I let out a howl, because the truth finally hits me.

Cousin Silas tries to grab me, but I fight him like a wildcat. My screeching brings the whole crowd around, except the Pathfinder, who's leaving in a carriage.

The crowd gapes at me like I'm an animal. And I am, because my pa's not here, and my big dream of what's to be just broke into a million pieces.

—Driver, give me a hand here!

The carriage driver jumps down, and the two of them pick me up, kicking and screaming, and put me in the carriage next to Cousin Opal, who squeezes my arms till I grow weak.

Then I just sit there, staring at the grey sky over the Mississippi.

The sun is gone. Thunder rolls in the distance as Silas yells at Cousin Opal.

—He's never coming back! He's tricked us into raising his half-breed mistake!

I clutch my Ma doll tight.

—*Don't believe him, Falling Star, don't believe him.*

But part of me does believe Cousin Silas – the part that feels so broken. On the ride back, my mind bumps and rolls like the carriage wheels over the cobblestones: Pa didn't tell the Pathfinder about me – didn't talk about me at all – was ashamed of me – didn't come for me – broke his promise – broke his word.

☆ ☆ ☆

Back at the house, Cousin Silas goes into a rage. His blood's up because he's so sure Pa tricked him. Drinking whiskey, he pretends to be Pa speaking.

—I know what I'll do! I'll let that fool Silas care for my Injun daughter, and I'll just go off and have a merry time like I always do. Get me some other squaw. Have me some more heathen kids! Send them all to my cousin Silas.

—Mama, is Adaline staying here for ever? Is she, Mama?

I'm outside the parlour window, close to the ground, hugging my bag of possibles, hoping my eagle feather, my dragonfly carving, my Ma doll, and Doc Hempstead's book on the Heavenly Bodies will keep me safe. Plus it's a fact that if you keep still, perfectly still, a grizzly's not so apt to pick you up and drag you off.

—She's not a bad worker, Silas.

—She's a savage, Opal. You saw her dancing and whooping like a hyena the other night.

—She was happy.

—When civilized people are happy, they don't act like that. Who wants a savage for a servant? Especially when we could get a good Irish or German orphan!

—I still think we can wash the Indian out of her.

—Yes, Mama! Scrub her till her skin turns white!

—Hush, Lilly.

—And throw away her devil doll!

—Lilly's right, Opal. Get rid of that hideous doll and all her Injun things.

—That's what I've been saying, Mama!

—It's a disgrace we ever let her heathen trinkets in this house.

—I'll get rid of them, Papa!

Lilly bangs out the kitchen door. She runs everywhere around the yard, her petticoats rustling.

I clutch my Ma doll.

—*We are in great danger, Little Frog. But you must be still. Do not try to hop away.*

I can't do what she says. I can't keep still. I feel like I'm caught in a trap – my tight corset and pinchy shoes don't help.

—Adaline! Adaline!

I stuff my Ma doll in my bag of possibles, then jump out of the bushes and dash across the grass.

Lilly shrieks when she sees me.

—There she is! Give me your doll, Adaline! Papa says so!

She tears after me.

I can't run fast enough in my shoes. And Caddie's blue bonnet falls off my head. When I go to grab it, I slip and fall.

Before I can jump back up, Lilly snatches my bag and runs off with it.

—I got it, Papa! I got it!

I scream and run after her. But Cousin Silas rushes between us and grabs me.

I push him off with the strength of a bear, then break for the house.

Lilly's inside. When I get to the parlour, she's standing by the fire, watching my things go up in flames.

I shove Lilly aside, then go to grab my Ma doll. But it's too late. Her head and chest are already burned away.

I moan and start to wail.

—Here, I didn't burn your book! A book's not a heathen thing!

Lilly holds up my book on the Heavenly Bodies.

—And your tinderbox – you can keep that.

Everything spins before my eyes. I make my way into the kitchen and grab a knife from the table.

Lilly screams.

Opal screams.

Cousin Silas runs for his gun.

I push past Lilly and Opal and veer outside with the knife. I crash into the bushes and grab chunks of my hair and saw them off. Then I run the blade of the knife over my arms and legs, and my blood streams down over Caddie's daughter's blue dress and my stockings and leather shoes and then I faint.

☆ ☆ ☆

—She was covered with blood, Reverend. My family and I have never witnessed such savagery before.

I open my eyes, then close them. I ain't with my ma. I didn't make it to the Land-Behind-the-Stars. Durn if I ain't still here, lying on my bed while Cousin Opal and Reverend Wallace stand near the door talking. I'm out of the bloody blue dress and wearing my nightgown. Rags are wrapped around my wounds. Caddie must have fixed me up.

—She has no other kin, Opal?

—No. She was abandoned by her father, Kit Carson, as you know. And her mother, a squaw-woman, died last spring.

—I see.

—Please understand, Reverend, we feel only

Christian love and kindness for the girl. But she is simply not capable of living with a civilized family. I've finally come to understand that.

—Then perhaps she belongs in the St Louis Orphan Home, Opal.

—Reverend, I fear she might use the knife against herself again. Or worse, against the other orphans. Lilly told me she recently tried to attack a group of small white children. I wish I had paid more attention.

—I'm sorry to say this, Opal, but it sounds as though she may belong in the insane asylum. They can restrain her passions there, keep her from hurting herself or anyone else.

Cousin Opal sighs.

—"Lost in the dark the heathen doth languish."

—Indeed. All we can do is pray for her, Opal. I'll have the asylum send a carriage tomorrow. Perhaps you'll want to keep Lilly from seeing her taken away. It might frighten your daughter if they have to put the girl in chains.

—Yes, poor Lilly's tried so hard to help her.

Their voices fade.

I open my eyes again. I'm alone. My room is almost dark. I look out my window and see the stars blink far away. I ache for my Ma doll. But she has turned to ashes now, sending my ma's spirit back to the Land-Behind-the-Stars.

And my pa's not coming today. Or any day.

And tomorrow I'm going to be put in chains.

I look hard at the distant stars, trying to see where my ma is. But Science tells me the stars are so plentiful, it might take me six hundred years to find her.

I squeeze my eyes shut and try to imagine what she would say to me if she still talked through my Ma doll.

At first all I hear is silence. Then I catch the faintest, softest words.

—*Hop away now, Little Frog. It is time.*

The house is dark and still. My knife wounds burn like fire, but they don't stop me from crawling under the bed and pulling out my buckskin clothes and the moccasins that Caddie let me save when I first came here.

It's my life I got to save now.

I pick up my bag of possibles. It feels right sorrowful, holding only my tinderbox and my book about the Heavenly Bodies. All my magic's gone up in smoke.

I need a knife and provisions. I limp out of my room to the kitchen. In my moccasins, I'm silent as a ghost. Only someone who hears the spirits would hear me.

The knife I cut myself with is on the wooden chopping block, washed clean of my blood. I pick it up and start to put it in my bag.

—Where you going with my butcher knife, child?

My heart stops. In the shadows I see Caddie standing in the doorway.

—You leaving them or scalping them?

I nod towards the outside.

—But what 'bout your wounds, child? You gonna hurt so bad.

I just keep looking at her, telling her with my eyes that nothing's going to stop me now.

—Long time ago, I run away, too. Me and my little girl run away. But she slipped off a bridge and drowned before I could get her. I buried her all by myself on the bank of the river, deep under the mud.

I stare at her, without breathing.

—When I got caught and sold to Mr Silas, I didn't tell nobody about her. Nobody here knows my little girl ever lived but you.

Caddie's secret drains the strength out of me. Neither of us says anything for a moment. Cricket sounds fill the air.

—I reckon you have to do it, though, child. You got no choice.

I don't know if I got the will to do it now. The world that killed Caddie's daughter seems unbearably sad.

—I'll get you something to eat.

She moves to the pantry and disappears for a moment. When she comes back, she's holding a bundle wrapped in a handkerchief.

—I put corn cakes and buckwheat cakes in here for you, and a piece of ham.

She puts the food bundle into my bag.

—And I *give* you my butcher knife. You'll need it.

She takes the knife out of my hand and adds it to the bag.

—Hurry now, before they come to lock you up.

I just stare at her.

—The moon's bright, so stay in the shadows. Follow the road a-ways, then head into the woods. Travel east and you'll come to a creek that'll take you to the Mississippi.

I nod. That's exactly what I want.

She puts her arms around me and squeezes me tight.

I squeeze her back, then give her hands a tug, urging her to come with me.

—I can't. I can't run again. I'm too old. Go now. Hurry –

She gives me a little push away from her and opens the back door.

—If you know how to fly, child, fly. Fly with the angels.

I slip outside, and the door closes gently behind me.

In the damp air, all the cobwebby bushes sparkle. I break past them and head for the road that leads to the woods. I hardly feel my wounds as I limp across the soggy grass, silent as a breath of wind.

I'm lucky Cousin Silas don't have a hundred dogs like the Arapaho. No captive could escape their camp without setting off a chorus of howls.

But nothing stirs here, except me and a hoot owl. We got the dark road all to ourselves.

I take off past the quiet houses, shedding my fears along the way.

Better to be lying half-dead in the wilderness,

waiting to be wolf meat, than lying in that civilized house, waiting to be chained.

Better to be limping all cut up through the darkness than waiting for ever for a pa who broke his word and ain't ever coming back.

All I got to do is find my way to the Mississippi—

—Whoa, who's that?

I freeze in my tracks.

Two men are coming up a side road. They're dressed like soldiers but weave like drunkards.

My heart thumps near out of my chest.

—It's an Injun boy, ain't it?

Wrong. Because I cut off my hair they got it wrong.

—I bet it's that wild Mohawk what knifed that family!

—Halt!

I break for the brush beside the road.

A shot rings out.

—Get him!

Another shot.

Oh, grief, that's what I get for thinking

proud thoughts and not keeping my eyes skinned for trouble!

—Shoot him!

I scramble past the brush and tear into the woods. I'm getting scraped and scratched and smacked by branches, but I just keep going faster.

I don't even feel the pain of my cuts. I just keep going and going. I fly like Caddie's angels are lifting me off the ground.

I move through the night woods for hours, till the moon's going down and the distant sky's a dark, sad grey.

Terrible tired, I finally come to a creek. White swirls of steam rise from the water. My wounds are bleeding and I feel like I'm about to give out. But I ain't stopping. I step right in the creek and keep going till I'm belly-deep in the cold, muddy water.

I hold my bag of possibles above my head, trying to keep *The Heavenly Bodies* dry. I feel the terrible burn of my knife cuts. But they don't really bother me.

The cold water don't bother me, either. Every morning when I was little, my ma would bathe me in the freezing creek, then let me dance naked in the grass.

I long to be with my ma – be with her in that faraway sky, that beautiful Land-Behind-the-Stars.

I'm in the creek water up to my neck now. Mist swirls around me. I can almost see the buffalo-skin tepees, the spotted ponies, the ghostlike shapes of the Arapaho.

I see Yellow Leaf and my ma dancing in the dusk, while the smoke from their fire curls up to the Great Holy Spirit, offering him their prayers.

It don't matter if my pa don't want me. If I climb the stairs to the Arapaho heaven, they'll let me in. They'll wrap a robe around my shoulders and feed me dried cherries mixed with buffalo marrow, then let me sleep on a cloud soft as feathers.

—*I'm comin', Ma!*

I close my eyes and wait for her answer. I wait and wait, but all I hear's the birds starting to greet the day.

I open my eyes again. The sun's creeping over the woods, casting an iron-red glow over the trees and creek and muddy bank.

Daylight's chasing away my Arapaho heaven. But I don't want to be caught by the daylight. I close my eyes again.

—*I'll find you, Ma! Even if it takes six hundred years!*

I'm about to let my arms drop, sink down with *The Heavenly Bodies*, let the water flow over my head and let my spirit depart and start marching up the ghost trail after my ma.

But then I hear a noise – something's rustling in the brush.

I open my eyes. My heart races. I'm willing to drown, but I ain't willing to get eaten by a bear.

Still holding my bag above my head, I try to reach in it for my knife.

An animal pokes its nose out from the bushes. It ain't a bear. It's a short-legged, crop-eared, mud-covered, scrawny critter, with a face like a muskrat.

It barks.

I'll be shot – it's a dog.

It barks again, then sits on the creek bank and watches me, real serious, with keen dark eyes.

Reckon I'll have to delay my trip to heaven.

I wade back to shore, keeping an eye on the dog. He just sits there, still as a lizard.

I set down my bag, not taking my eyes off him. He keeps staring back at me, too. Suspicious he might be more vicious than he lets on, I growl real low.

The scrawny varmint growls back, but a no-count growl, not mean enough to scare a rabbit.

Then he barks. I jump.

—I ain't afraid of you, dog!

Shoot, I just let go of my tongue and give away my first spoken words in six months to an ugly little dog!

And now he looks like he's laughing at me. His mouth's dropped open and he's panting, showing me his tongue.

I reckon he ain't vicious. But still I know one thing: he and I ain't going to be friends. Pa always says don't *never* take a dog on the trail. You get to caring too much about the critter and risk your life for him, or the very least, your future.

—Go away, dog. I don't need company.

He sort of wiggles his behind like he don't believe me.

—Go on, I said. Git. I mean it.

But the little mongrel keeps laughing like he still don't take me serious.

I turn away from him, determined not to look him in the eye again. I start prowling along the bank of the creek, scavenging for things to eat. I want to save Caddie's cakes and ham for when I'm starving.

The dog don't follow me, but I can feel he's watching my every move.

I find a log with some mushrooms growing on the side of it. It looks like the kind Yellow Leaf used to boil with buffalo meat. I pull out my knife and cut off a chunk.

When I bite down on it, it's tough as leather. I

don't have a pot to boil it in – but maybe I can soak it for a while and roast it later.

Suddenly I hear voices. I drop behind the log. My heart's pounding as I peer over the top and see a flatboat gliding down the creek through the milky air. I see a woman, a man, a young girl, some chairs, burlap bags, farming tools, a pig, a rooster. It looks like a dream. . .

I hear the murmur of their voices. The rooster spreads his wings. Then the boat drifts out of view.

I stand up. When I turn, I see the dog still staring after the boat with a look of deep yearning in his eyes.

Maybe he was travelling on this creek and fell off a boat just like that. Or maybe his people pushed him off and abandoned him. An ugly mongrel like him, who'd blame them?

He turns and looks at me with eyes so sad, it knocks the wind out of me, and I have to sit down on the log.

I put my head in my hands and all I see is black. Why didn't my pa tell the Pathfinder about me?

Why did he abandon me? And why won't my ma speak to me any more?

I feel the dog sniffing at me. When I wave my hands to shoo him away, he takes advantage and licks my face, and the next thing I know I'm a goner, blubbering because I ain't been kissed in a long time.

There's a lot of crying and licking till I finally get the strength to push him back from me.

—Git away, you.

Then we look at each other, dog eye to wet human eye.

So much for my freedom.

Durn if he didn't slip into my heart as swift and sneaky as a Pawnee arrow.

And now all the stupid birds are singing like they've been enjoying the show.

—Don't be too happy, birds. Because I ain't going to love him. I promise.

—This creek must be the one Caddie told me about. It'll take us to the Mississippi River, and that'll take us to the Missouri River.

I'm talking to the dog while I peel the rags off my cuts and splash water on them.

—If I follow the Missouri, I'll end up at Kansas Landing, just where I want to be. There I'll hook up with some traders heading back to Bent's Fort.

He stares at me without blinking. My wounds are killing me. I got to keep talking to bear it.

—It's getting near October now. Arapaho call that the Moon-When-the-Water-Begins-to-Freeze-on-the-Edge-of-the-Stream.

The dog's nose twitches, like he's trying to smell the meaning of my words.

—I used to live in two places. Pa's rooms at

Bent's Fort where he was a trapper. And my grandpa's tepee on Horse Creek where I was born.

The dog tilts his head.

—My pa was a scout for the Fremont expedition. And my ma's up there.

I point to the Land-Behind-the-Stars.

But the dog stares at my hand.

—No, not here. Lookee there. *Up* there.

As I wag my finger, the dog comes over and licks it.

—Oh, git away from me, fool.

I sit on the bank, weary. My cuts hurt bad. And in the last few minutes, the sun's gotten real hot.

Kerplop.

I look around. The dog's swimming away.

—Where you going?

He climbs ashore further down the creek, shakes fast and hard, then moves on down the bank.

—Hey dog! Where you going?

He keeps moving like a little fox gliding through the grass. Then he disappears, dipping behind some weeds at the edge of the water.

I don't hear nothing.

—Hey, where'd you go?

I move down the bank, then push aside some tall weed stalks.

And there he is, sitting on the bank next to something that looks like a canoe.

It *is* a canoe! An old canoe made of bunches of rushes tied to a frame of willow sticks. It's even got a wooden paddle!

I whoop. By grief, it's as good as finding the Baby Moses in the bulrushes. Now I got a way to get up to the Mississippi.

I push the dog aside and get to work digging out all the leaves and dirt that's settled in the hollow. I use a twig to clear the cobwebs.

Then I stand up. I take a deep breath and shove the canoe off the sand with a run. Once it's in the water, I jump over the end and grab the paddle and start paddling.

It's a miracle! This stick floats! I'm so happy I holler like a Pawnee.

When I look over my shoulder, I see the dog on the bank staring at me. He don't look happy at all.

I stop paddling.

—Hey, what's the matter? You think I was going to leave you? Shoot, you found the durn thing.

I paddle back over to the bank.

—Come on. Git in.

I haul his skinny little body into the front of the canoe, where I'd thrown my bag of possibles.

He sneezes. Then he just sits there and smiles at me, his tongue out.

—Now don't bother anything. Just sit there.

The sun is singing as I push off again. Hawks circle overhead against a blue sky.

We both sit in silence as I paddle us up the creek. We're paddling against the wind, and that don't make it easy for us.

Actually *I'm* the one doing all the paddling. He's just sitting there like the Queen of Sheba. It's a perfect dog's life. No wonder he's grinning and I ain't.

—This is pretty hard when you ain't had nothing to eat and you run all night without any sleep and you got bloody cuts all over your arms and legs. I don't know how long I can do it.

He ain't even listening, though, he's sniffing the air.

—What? You think you smell some daisies? You want me to stop and pick them and weave you a little crown?

I'm about to complain some more when he barks real low, like he's saying, *Be quiet, pay attention.*

I get quiet and hear a hum of voices coming from up the creek.

Now the dog stares at me like he's saying, *See, while you was yapping your fool-talk, I was working at smelling.*

I paddle quick-like under the dead leaves and branches of an uprooted tree that's hanging over the bank. We wait.

A fish slaps the water. The voices get closer.

The dog's breathing a little too loud for my peace of mind. But try and make a critter like that hold his breath.

There now – they're coming.

Four men on a raft slide past our hiding place.

I can't see their faces all that well. But their clothes tell me they're fur traders – they're decked out in buckskin and their flatboat's loaded with bales of fur to take to St Louis.

Their talking is music to my ears:

—Yessiree, I tickled that old blind bear's hump ribs with my flat knife and said, You ain't eating me this morning, stranger.

—I got one better 'n that, Bill. One summer at Green River, I danced a polka with a one-armed grizzly.

—Naah, you did not.

—You ask Black Harris – or ask the bear herself. She'll tell you. . .

They all laugh.

Sounds like the talk I heard all my life in Rosalie's kitchen at Bent's Fort. I reckon they must be coming from upriver, from the Missouri.

We listen till their talking and laughing fades away into the distance.

The familiar sound and smell of those traders has made me thirsty to find somebody . . . and you know who I mean. I talk low to the dog.

— After I git to the fort, I'll set out to find Pa. I'll grab him by the ears, look him eyeball to eyeball, and ask him: why didn't you tell John C. Fremont about me? Are you ashamed of me?

The dog looks woeful. His eyes don't blink.

—That's all I'm living for now.

I push us out of the shadows and start paddling hard up the creek again.

The dog sneezes, like he's relieved to move on.

I'm thinking to push on even after nightfall. But at twilight, rain-smelling clouds cover us and a strong wind tries to blow us back from where we come.

I figure the Thunderbird's about to fly over, and sure enough, a flash of fire zigzags across the sky. There's a loud crack. The dog starts barking.

As I quick paddle us to the bank of the creek, raindrops start pinging onto the water. Pretty soon I'm getting drenched.

The dog jumps out of the canoe and barks impatiently near a thicket of wild plum at the edge of the creek.

—Keep your britches on.

By the time I lug the canoe into the thicket, the

rain's coming down so hard, it's taking the hide off me.

When I turn back around, the dog's gone.

—Hey! Where'd you go?

A boom that sounds like the end of creation shakes the earth. I leap like a rabbit hit by a cannonball and fall into the water weeds.

I lie there some seconds like I'm dead, but I guess I ain't because I'm able to wonder if I am.

I hold up my head. No, I ain't dead. But where's that durn dog?

Soaked to the bone, I stagger to my feet and holler for him.

—Dog! Dog!

I picture him burnt up by that lightning bolt or lying squashed somewhere under a fallen tree.

I holler again and again, running around in circles, getting more and more soaked by the rain.

—Dog! *Dog!*

Durn if Pa's words ain't come true already. You take a dog on the trail and pretty soon you're bound to make a fool of yourself.

—DOG!

The grass moves.

—Dog?

Yep. He wiggles out from behind a bush, smiling like he does.

Then all of a sudden the wind stops. And the rain. Completely. It's like the Thunderbird was ordered to move on, like the Lord said, *Peace, be still, and the wind ceased and there was great calm.*

A rainbow arches through the sky. Yellow Leaf would say the Thunderbird was now casting his fishing line down through the clouds.

The dog barks at me, then moves off quickly, leading us to a good camping spot. Leading us kindly, like a light in the gloom.

—Git back.

I'm so tired and sore, I can hardly unwrap the cakes and ham Caddie gave me. And the dog ain't helping. He's found us a shelter under a drippy willow, and now he's pawing my arm, poking out his nose, looking to share my dinner.

—Git back, I said.

He stares politely as I take a bite. But his mouth is half open, and spit drops from it.

—Aw grief! This is another reason why I shouldn't have let you come with me.

I offer him a piece of my cake and he swallows it in one fat gulp.

—Don't you know how to find your own provisions?

He looks at me like he don't.

I give him the last of my ham. I'm too tired to pick a fight.

Then I lie down, feeling terrible pain from my knife wounds. He lies next to me, his behind against my chest.

I'm too achy to push him away. So I'm forced to put my arm around him.

—Just don't give me no fleas.

Now the cold's creeping in, so I'm forced to press my face against his fur to keep my nose warm.

—Don't get no ideas. We ain't staying this way all night.

But in a second, we're asleep and we sleep so hard we don't even dream.

When we wake up, the sun's glancing off the weeds; birds are singing carefree.

The dog raises his head and yawns, then looks at me, his eyes wide. *Ready?*

I'm mighty sore as I sit up. My cuts feel even worse than the day before.

He keeps looking at me, his head tilted.

—OK, OK.

Even though I'm aching, a sudden joy fills me. More canoeing ahead. Plenty of time and sunlight.

Freedom is the best thing to hoard in your bag of possibles. Today freedom is taking Caddie's kitchen knife and carving the point of a stick into a fishing spear. It's standing on the bank of the creek and aiming for a shad – getting it, thanking it, then cooking it after you make a fire with flint from your tinderbox.

Freedom's watching the blue smoke rise into the morning light while you share your fresh-caught feast with a dog who's mighty grateful, then washing it down with a little rainwater from the hollow of your canoe.

Freedom is putting out your fire, erasing all your signs and tracks, then pushing that canoe on to a sparkling creek with the waters high from the storm, and the sky above the colour of gooseberries before they're ripe.

We ain't seen any keelboats or flatboats all day. Must be because it's Sunday.

There may not be any boats on this river, but there sure are plenty of mosquiters. The Rain Spirits last night begat hoards of them, critters so big they could drill holes in your pots. And now it seems they're all right *here*, biting *me*.

But the dog don't seem to mind. His eyes shine like new money. He's grinning at me, tongue out, like he's saying, *It's just a bunch of little old mosquiters. What kind of scout are you?*

He don't know my cuts hurt like the devil. I got fresh bloodstains on my leggings. But what's most worrisome is that the knife wound down my left arm is looking red and raw, and that arm is right much bigger than it ought to be.

I'm easy prey for the mosquiters. And by grief, now we're about to glide right into a whole throbbing cloud of the bloodthirsty critters! They're humming so loud, it sounds like screaming.

Before I get eaten alive, I pull off my moccasins and leap out of the canoe into the creek.

When I bob up for air, the dog's looking ready to jump, too – and he *does* – right in my face.

I'm flapping around like a goose while he's looking more like a muskrat than ever with his wet fur face, his short legs paddling. I have to laugh, even in my misery.

Then I see our canoe gliding away down the creek, my moccasins and bag of possibles with it!

The dog and I swim after it. But it ain't so easy for me in my soaked buckskins with my bad arm – or for him, either, with his stubby little legs.

We get lucky, though, because the canoe drifts over to the bank and gets caught in some weeds.

We drag ourselves out of the water. The dog gives a good shake and rubs his nose in the grass while I haul the canoe into dry brush.

My buckskins are soggy and heavy as I pull on my moccasins. All of a sudden, I feel like my legs are about to give out. I have to sit.

The dog crouches nearby, snapping at the air, trying to catch the mosquiters and flies.

Dang critters are still thirsty for my blood, but I can't think about them now. I got something worse to ponder. I got a fever from my cuts. I'm starting to shake, feeling hot and cold at the same time.

I've seen the results of poisoned wounds. I've seen trappers die or go lame from them. I look the dog in the eye.

—A friend of Pa's once got gangrene in his arm from a bullet wound. Pa had to saw the feller's arm off with a razor. Then he pressed a fire-hot wagon bolt against the bloody stump to seal it off.

The dog tilts his head like I'm joking.

—I ain't joking. But you know what? That feller was ready to ride the next day.

The dog looks doubtful.

—It's true. And I seen Doc Hempstead saw limbs and press fire to them, too.

I shudder, shaking off thoughts of razors and hot wagon bolts. I need Arapaho medicine. I haul myself up, then start weaving around the bank, looking for a tree. There's plenty of trees around, of course, but it's got to be the right one.

I find a young pine.

—Thankee, Tree Spirit, for your power to heal me.

I pull out my knife and work off some green bark. I use what's left of my strength to pound the bark with a rock till it's soft. Then I look for a cobweb to fix my blood.

When I find one, I thank the speckled brown spider what made it and drape her sticky threads across my wound. Using one hand, my teeth, and Caddie's handkerchief, I tie the bark and cobweb around my arm.

There. But now I'm so worn out, I slip down into the leaves and curl up into a ball. My whole body's got the trembles.

The dog watches serious-like. When he tries to get close, I tell him not to.

—Git back, you ugly mudpie.

He's filthy dirty from the creek.

It's just about twilight now. Shadows are covering the bank.

I'm in a shaky fix here. But I asked for it. I made these cuts myself and now I'm reaping the reward.

I try to figure out what else Running-in-a-Circle would do. I've seen him use skunk oil and bear grease on bloody wounds, racoon fat, too. But I ain't got the strength to go hunting critters now.

Night covers us so thick, I don't see a single star in the sky. But all the time I know the dog's near. I can hear him breathe, hear him flick away the wing-whines of mosquiters.

Don't leave me, I tell him. Don't leave like my pa and my ma left. But he don't even try. He sits close all night as I drift in and out of sleep.

Night creeps off, but the sun never rises. All through the grey morning, my arm screams with pain. I start to dream that wolves are gnawing on it and ants are crawling on my flesh. As buzzards swoop down to peck out my eyes, I jerk awake.

I can't keep lying out here in the open.

I clutch my bag of possibles. The dog stays near me as I pull myself over snakelike roots, through bunches of leaves, rattling them like a windstorm.

We move and rest, move and rest, until I finally get myself under the shelter of a swaying willow tree and fall asleep again.

I wake at twilight, hidden by the tree's weepy branches. Now I hear singing and whispering. I hear the beating of a drum and someone chanting *hay-a-hay.*

I see Running-in-a-Circle behind the ripple of the willow leaves, sifting the white powdered bone of a giant fish. I hear him whisper about the magic of the mud turtle's shell and the hide of the weasel.

It gets darker and darker, and the drumbeat and chanting get louder. Then Pa's shaking me, in a rage because I slashed myself up again. Running-in-a-Circle lies on his buffalo robe. Pa shouts, How's he going to help you if he can't help hisself? I hear the wind blowing over Horse Creek, blowing in the dark, over scorched earth and bleached bones. Where is everyone? They're all dead. I know it.

Blackness covers everything.

Am I dead, too?

I reach out for the dog in a panic. He presses his head against my open hand and licks my trembly fingers.

When my ma died, the Arapaho burned her bed and all her clothes. They killed her white horse, too, so she could ride his spirit on her long journey over the trail of ghosts.

It don't seem right I got only this no-count critter to walk to heaven with. It seems we ain't got a choice, though. We've already started up that path.

But then the dog pulls away from me and stands up like he's made a big decision.

In the black night, he starts licking my head. I'm too weak to push him away. And he keeps licking till I think he's about to lick my ear off. He licks and licks and licks, the way a mother dog licks her new puppy into being.

Lightning flashes. Wolves howl. Bald-headed

eagles scream in the sky. I know now for sure the Arapahos sent me a helping spirit. Come with the force of a holy whirlwind, he's whispering in my ear, *Live, live, live.*

Then the dang dog sits down against me and puts his muddy head on my chest. I feel his heart thumping – and it feels like it's beating in time with mine, making it strong enough to get me through the night. I don't know where he begins and I end. I don't care if he's ugly or muddy. As long as this mongrel stays with me, my flame will keep on burning.

Thirst wakes me. The sun's streaming golden green through the willow branches, and the good news is, no wolf ate my arm, no buzzard pecked out my eye. I ain't dead. And I feel right much better.

My fever seems to have broke with the sunrise. And the poison in me is gone for sure, I can tell. Maybe my luck's turned.

—Hey!

I just got licked on the mouth.

I take hold of the dog's little ears and look him nose to nose. He's got an ugly face, but I'm mighty glad to see it.

—Were you a messenger of the Great Holy Spirit last night?

In the swaying light and shadows he seems just

a fool panting dog, and I have to say his breath ain't all that divine.

I let go of him and sit up. It's a fact: I'm better. I ain't shaking, my cuts ain't hurting. Well, maybe a little bit. But not nearly like the last two days.

Stranger still, when I peel Caddie's handkerchief off my arm and my poultice falls to the ground, I see that cut ain't so red and raw-looking any more. My arm ain't swollen so much, neither, and my other cuts are looking better, too.

I crawl out from under the willow and try to stand, but weakness brings me back to my knees. I hold my head in my hands, feeling like the woods are spinning.

No, I ain't perfect yet. I don't know how I'm ever going to get the strength to catch me a fish. But I'm so all-fired thirsty, I do know one thing: I got to drink some water or die.

I use all my strength to get up. Once I'm on my feet, I'm determined to stay there. I stagger down to the bank with the dog at my heels.

I kneel beside the creek. It's as still as glass.

When I see my reflection, I can't believe it's me. With my hair chopped so close to my head, I really do look like a wild Indian boy. No wonder those drunk soldiers thought I was the murdering Mohawk.

I scoop some water into my hands and throw it on my face. Then I take a sip, hoping it's clean enough not to make me sick.

I decide to try some more Arapaho medicine. I pick some chickweed near the bank and mash it with a rock. Then I wash my wounds with creek water and rub them with the mashed-up weed.

The dog whines from down the bank a-ways.

I look up. He noses the grass and whines some more.

It ain't like him to whine, so I haul myself up and stagger over to him.

Durn if he ain't standing over a big fish, flopping on the bank – a real big one, big enough for both our breakfasts! It's almost like that fish flopped himself out of the creek just to keep us from starving. Our luck's changed for sure!

I kneel down and thank the fish for sacrificing his

life to feed us. Then I find a rock and send his ghost to the Great Holy Spirit, leaving his flesh behind.

I get my knife from my bag and cut off his head and clean him. I gather some dry twigs and rub my flints together till I get my kindling going.

Then I find a flat stone, place it close to the fire, and put the fish on it to roast. Some of it we'll eat now. Some I'll smoke till it's dried out and we can have it for supper later.

Even though I'm still weak and my arm is right sore, I pick some wild onion roots and sassafras leaves to add to our meal.

The smoke curls into the cool air and a pair of ducks sets down on the misty creek.

As we share our breakfast and drink more water, we watch the ducks sail upstream over a path of sunlight shimmering like gold dust.

With food in me now, I'm aching to get back on that sparkly path myself. I look the dog in the eye.

—Ready to ride?

He sneezes.

The day's so fresh and cool, the mosquiters seem

to have gotten disgusted with these parts and gone elsewheres to make trouble.

In the early morning haze, we slip in and out of the shade, gliding north. The turtles leave their sunny rocks and plop into the water. Birds pipe, one by one, then all together.

My ma used to predict the weather by the song of the birds. I wish I could ask her right now what's coming next. She could speak from a rock or a bush. But she don't.

My arm ain't hurting too bad now. I'm sure we won't be having the water all to ourselves once we get closer to the Mississippi. So I paddle us over to the bank that's most dense with forest, trying to keep us hidden.

The dog sits in front of the canoe, staring at me, sleepy-like.

—I'm heading out to find my pa. Did I tell you that?

He yawns.

—When I get to Bent's Fort, I'll get me a horse and ride to New Mexico. Then one day I'll jump out from behind a bush – Ha! Found you at last!

The dog lifts his head and sniffs. I ain't sure he's listening, but I go right on.

—He said he loved me like an old squirrel loves a nut. Now I know those were just pretty words.

The dog gives me that low bark of his, like he's saying, *Stop yer yapping, fool, and pay attention. This creek's about to join up with the Mississippi.*

He's right. As we slide along the curvy shore, under the mossy hanging trees, the creek grows wider by the minute, and pretty soon we're on a rushing yellow river.

Here, the turtles look bigger, the birds sing louder.

The dog settles back down and stretches out. His eyes close. Soon he's twitching and whining, like he's dreaming about finding that big fish what jumped ashore to feed us.

He don't think he's the Queen of Sheba like I first thought. I'm happy to let him sleep all he wants now, since he worked so hard last night to pull me back from the Valley of the Shadow of Death.

☆ ☆ ☆

The first signs of Mississippi River civilization come mid-afternoon, when we see a pair of log cabins tucked back in the woods. There's chickens scratching in the dirt, and a goat eating the tall grass down by the yellow river.

We're lucky no one is standing outside the cabins to see us as we slip by. Wearing my dirty buckskins, I'm scared I'm going to be mistaken for that crazy Mohawk again. I'm wishing I had some other clothes.

When we get a good ways past the cabins, I paddle into a hidden spot under a willow tree to rest.

There I tell the dog something else that's on my mind.

—Might astonish you to know I'm a girl.

He don't look too astonished.

—But as my hair's chopped off, I'd like to keep passing for a boy. Folks don't think it's all that strange to see a boy on his own.

He nods his head in a manner almost human. Or maybe he's just dodging a fly.

Even though we're out of the sun, the air feels thick and hazy. I lean back and tell him about the Arapaho boys at Horse Creek.

—If I was one of them, I'd have to grow up and be a warrior – decorate my body with eagle feathers, dance the secret Sun Dance. Some of them torture themselves during that dance to show how brave they are. They hang themselves from a pole by leather thongs pulled through their chest muscles. I could do that. I'm brave enough.

The dog snorts.

—I'm not kidding.

The dog don't seem to care. He jumps up and stares hard at the river.

I stare with him and catch sight of a keelboat coming into view. We stay frozen, hidden by the droopy willow branches.

The keelboat's piled high with furs. About ten strong-looking men are holding long poles and walking the boat down the river.

The dog and me don't move till they've disappeared from our view. Then I whisper my thoughts to him.

—They were coming from the north, probably from the Missouri. We must be getting close.

I paddle us out of our shady cove, and we glide up the river. We stay close to the shore, so we can hide again if we need to.

When we round a bend, I catch my breath. There's not just *signs* of civilization ahead – but civilization her very self.

On the top of a slope above the river is a big white mansion with a verandah and huge columns and a fancy flower garden that leads down to a boat landing. Near the landing three boys are playing in the water.

We hug the shade on our woody side of the river and watch them.

They don't see us because they're having too much fun, hollering and jumping around in the long shadows of the late afternoon.

I can't make out their exact words, but all at once, they start swimming down the river. They're splashing with a fury, like they're having a race. And they've left all their clothes behind, strewn across the wooden landing.

I don't know who has the idea first, me or the dog. But when we look at each other, I see his eyes twinkling and it's decided.

We wait as the three boys swim further and further downriver, till they're out of sight.

Then I paddle as hard as I can over to shore.

I slide into the yellow water, then wade knee-deep to the landing. In a flash, I grab a hat, a shirt, and a pair of britches, first ones I can get my hands on.

The dog's standing in the canoe on all fours, smiling, as I splash back to him, holding the goods high above my head.

—Got 'em! Let's go!

I hear the boys' happy yelling way in the distance as I paddle up the river as quick as I can.

The sun's gone down by the time we make camp in a thicket of wild plum and hazel.

I examine the shirt and britches I stole. They're both made out of heavy brown cloth, still shiny and smooth with not a tear or a stain anywhere.

I peel off my dirty, bloodstained buckskins and wash myself in the river, using Caddie's handkerchief to scrub all the dried blood off my arms and legs. My cuts are starting to scab over now and that's a good sign.

When I try on the shirt, it's a little big, but I roll up the sleeves and it don't seem too bad. When I step into the britches, they're too big, too, but I reckon the suspenders will keep them from falling off.

The hat fits perfectly fine.

I stand up straight. There. In a flicker of twilight, I've become a proper-dressed boy.

The dog don't look too impressed. But I feel like I just doubled my protection.

—See, it's OK now for us to paddle through crowded waters. If I wave polite, I can pass for a half-breed boy who's been civilized.

The dog ain't listening. He scratches the dirt to make a bed, turns around a few times, and plops down.

—And if I sit on the bank of the river, reading my book on the Heavenly Bodies, I'll look like a half-breed boy who's been civilized *and* educated.

He sighs, bored-like, then rolls over on his side and closes his eyes.

—Wait and see. They might ask me to run for president.

But he's asleep now. His little ribs show as his stomach rises and falls with each breath.

—Hey, you. Wake up. You forgot to eat.

His eyes open.

I pull our dried fish out of my bag, and he's up in a flash.

I take out my knife and cut the fish in two. I hold out his half and it's gone in a gulp.

—Good.

I'm worried about his little ribs showing like that.

In the morning, I'll catch us some more.

He lies back down on his side.

—You OK?

He opens one eye.

Yeah, he's OK.

Me, too. I lie down beside him in my new boy's clothes. I put my arm around him. And even before the buffalo stars come out, we two mongrels are sound asleep.

I stare at the early sky as the last stars linger, about to be chased off by daylight. The dog and I are head to head, both on our backs. He's snoring like he does.

I give him a nudge.

—Hey, skinnybones. Wake up. We gotta get to the Missouri.

He opens his eyes, rolls over and stares at me.

—Know what else? I got to fatten you up. Don't like the way your ribs poke out.

I kiss the top of his ugly head. Then I stand up and brush off my shirt and britches and pull on my hat.

The dog stretches and gives himself a good shake. I wish I could shake myself like that – so quick and complete. Shake off bad times and bad dreams.

In the pale dawn light, he tags behind me down to the river. Little wispy clouds are piled up in the sky to the north. I wonder how my ma would read them.

—Will it be windy? Will it rain?

Of course, she don't answer me.

And today, no fish seems ready to sacrifice itself to keep us from starving. I reckon the Great Holy Spirit only sends that kind of miracle when you're desperate.

I find some wild apples along the bank, but they're so wormy, they ain't worth nothing. As I'm rooting around for something else, I catch a sight that makes my eyes bug out: fresh bear tracks.

The foot's about the size of mine, spread out wide, with claw points on each toe. The tracks go for a few feet over the mud, then vanish at the water's edge.

If Pa were here, he'd not only name the age and mood of the critter, he'd tell you if its stomach was full, if it had a hurt tooth or blind eye. My pa's so good on the trail, he can read all the signs and sounds of nature. But I'm not bad myself. Looking at these tracks, I'd say this particular bear is a might smaller than me, and he's done left the bank and swum away.

Still, we ain't sticking around.

The dog's at my heels as I hurry to where the canoe is. I pull it out of the brush. As I drag it towards the water, I hear a noise and look up.

By grief, a black bear's standing on his hind legs at the edge of the woods, not fifteen metres away. I was wrong about where he went, and worse, I was wrong about his size – he's taller than my pa! His eyes flash as he looks straight at us.

I feel such a shock, I freeze solid. But when the bear starts to step toward us, I thaw out and get moving.

The dog barks, but I scoop him up and throw him into the canoe. He keeps barking and barking.

I'm almost in the canoe myself, when I realize I left my bag of possibles on the bank, on the other side of that varmint! I can't leave it – it's got our flint and my book on the Heavenly Bodies.

I push the canoe into the water so the dog's safe.

The bear stares at me, raking the air with his claws, as I move slow-like up on to the bank. Then I pick up a stone and toss it into the river, making a splash like a fish flopping.

When the bear turns to look, I fly past him to my bag and snatch it up.

But that bear ain't fooled for long. The next second he looks back and starts lumbering towards me. I ain't got no choice. I scream like a screech hawk, then pick up a stick and run straight towards the varmint. I poke him in the snout. He steps back, surprised-like, and I roar on past him into the river and splash out to the canoe.

As I climb aboard, the bear gets really mad and starts into the water himself. The dog's barking his fool head off. I grab my paddle and start paddling faster than I've ever paddled, faster than I thought I could paddle. I'm moving so fast through the mist, I don't seem human, especially a human just brought back from the door of death. But I move like the wind and don't look back.

When I finally do, the bear's gone. I put down

my paddle and take a long, deep breath. Then another. And another.

I look at the dog.

—Well, I'm sorry me and that critter didn't get the chance to dance. I know I could have licked him.

The dog smiles at me, like he's glad we're going to by lying to each other for miles to come.

As we glide up the river, we're pretty well hid by the morning mist. I'm still wondering what we're going to eat today. I got to keep up my strength so I don't get weak and slip into a fever again.

The dog's gazing dreamy-eyed over the side of the canoe, while I'm looking for a good place to stop and fish.

I could try to get one with my bare hands. Or I could find the right stick and carve a spear like I did two days ago. Or I could make a net and scoop up a whole bunch in one big swoop. That's a trick I learned from the Arapaho.

Here's how you do it:

1. Pull your canoe over to a woody little island in the middle of the river.
2. Get out, and while the dog sits on the bank watching, cut down about ten little bushes.
3. Find the longest vine you can. Cut it down with your knife.
4. Use the vine to tie all your little bushes together in a row, so you've got a nice bushy net about three metres long.
5. Give one end of your vine to the dog and tell him to hold it in his mouth.
6. The dog won't want to hold his end, so take it away from him.
7. Tie the dog's end of the vine around a little sapling a couple of metres from shore.
8. Wade into the river, holding the other end of your net.
9. Drag the net through the water.
10. Keep dragging for a very long time, till your net starts to come apart and you realize this ain't going to work.

I decide to make me another spear. After a long time carving and a long time stabbing the water, I catch three puny catfish. Two to eat now and one for later.

By the time I'm done with the whole business of catching and cooking those fish, sharing them with the dog, gathering pawpaws, digging up roots and rubbing my wounds with fresh chickweed, half a day's gone.

We're resting on a rock before heading up the river. You could change the word *mist* to *fog* now. It hovers around us, keeping us pretty well hid if any flatboats come by.

The dog's curled up, snoring. Why not? Doubtless he's exhausted from watching me paddle so fast and fish so hard.

While he rests, I chew on some cedar bark to help clear out any poison left in my wounds. Then I pull out my book on the Heavenly Bodies. I figure I ought to read it a little, since I risked my durn life this morning to save it.

Some astronomers believe there
are an unlimited number of stars
in the sky, continuing into infinity.

I know *infinity* means for ever, world without end. So if the stars continue into infinity, I have to inquire again: where is the Land-Behind-the-Stars? If these fellers are right, it ain't going to take just six hundred years to find it. It's going to take for ever.

I'm glad it ain't night-time. If I was to ponder this answer before sleep, I'd be mighty low-spirited, lying under the stars, unable to escape the meaning of it all. But right now, at midday, I can just shove the knowledge of Science back in my bag, stand up, and clap my hands.

—Let's git!

The dog's up real fast. Nice thing about dogs, they doze a lot, but in a shout, they're right back on their feet.

We erase all our signs and tracks and get back in the canoe. The fog is so thick as I paddle us north that it's hard to see the banks of the river.

But it don't really matter, because all we seem to be passing is ghosty black forest on both sides. There's nothing moving on the river but us. We're all alone, gliding through a watery silence.

My thoughts float to where we're headed . . . Rosalie's kitchen at Bent's Fort. I picture Rosalie serving me and Doc some corn cakes and molasses while we swap stories about all the happenings since I've been gone. When I get wind of Pa's exact whereabouts in New Mexico, I'll borrow a horse, then set out. A hundred Blackfoot warriors won't stop me from hunting him down.

We glide for most of the afternoon. Then the dog looks alert and his tail starts to wag.

Through the fog, I see a cotton field with slaves working . . . a grove of fruit trees . . . parts of a plantation spread. It's like we're travelling through a dream.

Then we see a flatboat piled high with hay, moving through the white haze . . . then another piled with logs.

We hear a bell ringing. And I sense something mighty big's about to happen. The dog seems to sense it, too, because his ears are up and he's staring hard into the fog.

We both wait and stare, and the air gets cleaner, like the sun's been ordered to burn away the haze, just so's we can see the big change that's about to take place.

As it gets more clear, I see we've moved into a wider part of the river, so wide it would be hard to stand on one side and shoot an arrow to the other.

I have a feeling we've left the Mississippi now and found our way to the Missouri.

Then, all at once, we see the big event rounding the bend: a steamboat. She's got two tall chimneys belching out streams of black smoke; huge paddle wheels, coloured flags flying; and folks standing at the railings, wearing beaver hats and bonnets.

Her bell rings again.

The dog starts barking, like he's saying, *Move! Move! We're in the way!*

And he's right! She's coming straight for us!

I start paddling for the bank. The current's stronger now.

The steamboat bell clangs again and again. Folks along the rail have spotted me and are cheering me on as I paddle crazy-like to get out of the way.

—Paddle, boy!

—Faster! Faster!

—Look at him go!

Huge ripples almost flip us over as we near the bank. By the time me and the dog scramble ashore, the steamboat's moved on downriver, and my moment of glory is over.

We hide our canoe in a tangle of brush, then hide ourselves under some hanging moss and catch our breath.

As the sun goes down, we see another steamboat – this one headed *up* the Missouri like us.

She's a gleaming palace with a thousand lights blazing on her three decks, casting shimmering reflections on the river. Her black smoke billows into the sky, like Arapaho pipe smoke, blending with the twilight clouds.

I can hear cheerful piano and fiddle music and see the silhouettes of folks leaning against the railing on the top deck. At this moment, there's no one on this earth I'd rather be than one of them.

—I wish we could hitch a ride on a steamboat. But I don't know how.

The dog tilts his head and gives me a serious look.

—I reckon we could sneak aboard. But they'd catch us, sure. Probably send me back to Cousin Silas.

He sighs, impatient-like.

—You know what?

He sticks his nose out and blinks.

—We could buy us a ticket.

He shakes his whole self, as if my foolishness surpasses belief.

—You think that's crazy?

He loses interest, lies down, and shuts his eyes.

But I'm lost in my yearning. Why, if me and Pa were on that boat now, we'd be on the top deck, feeling the breeze under the first stars. We'd step into the saloon and watch the fine ladies and soldiers swirl to the piano music all a-glitter in the candlelight.

But there's no hope of me and this dog ever getting a ride on a fancy boat like that. We're left in her wake as shimmering ripples spread out behind her like a swallow's wings.

The dog sits up and puffs at me, asking if we can turn our attention to supper.

I give him the fish I saved, and I eat the chicory roots and pawpaws I gathered at noon.

By-and-by, the moon rises over the opposite side of the bank. The wind moves among the trees, making their branches rattle. Ghostlike mist wafts over the black water. The night seems alive with spirits.

I ain't spooked, of course. But I worry the dog might be. I put my arm around him. Then, for his sake, I pray aloud to the Great Holy Spirit to protect us from all invisible things. In case he's still scared, I sing him one of Rosalie's favourite hymns:

Look, ye saints, the sight is glorious.
Crown Him!
Crown Him! Crowns become the victor's brow!

I guess I'm dreaming because that big black bear's coming at us again. Only this time, the old fool asks me and the dog to dance. Soon the three of us is whirling around the floor of the steamboat saloon, going 'round and 'round to that happy music. By the time the moon goes down, we're all purty near best friends.

The sun's casting long shadows when we finally stand up and stretch. A couple of deer drink from the water's edge. It's a pretty day with birds singing and a cool breeze blowing the tangled tree mosses.

I figure we'll push off early, then stop upriver a-ways to fish for breakfast. But I change my mind about that plan when I go to get our canoe.

The reason – it's gone.

I run up and down the water's edge, thinking it might have drifted a little and got trapped in the weeds. I squint hard at the river, wondering if it slid off with the current. For a moment, I think I see it, then realize I'm just looking at a fallen log. I finally have to admit to myself that it's gone.

The loss of that canoe takes the wind out of me. I sit on the bank and ponder what could have happened. The breeze ain't blowing that hard. The deer didn't take it, and I can't picture nobody sneaking through the grass, looking for something to steal.

Which just leaves the Ghost Spirits we sensed in the dark. It makes you shiver to think of them. Leastwise, me. The dog don't seem to mind at all. In the clear light of day, dogs seem to forget the night.

The fact is, it don't matter who or what took it. We ain't got no choice now but to walk. We weren't making such good time anyway. If we can just stay out of sight and keep following the river, we'll eventually get to Kansas Landing.

I grab my bag of possibles, pull off my moccasins, and start tramping through the river weeds.

When I look back, the dog's just staring at me, his eyes curious.

—Well, come on!

He sneezes, then scampers after me. Another thing I've noticed about dogs – they greet all new adventures with a sneeze.

By-and-by, we come upon a patch of wild

strawberries. I stop to pick some while the dog tries to slop up minnows at the water's edge.

He ain't having much luck, so I have to take the time to help him with a spear, then make a quick campfire to cook him a catfish. I have to say, he seems mighty grateful and gives good warning a little while later when he sees a snake slithering through the weeds, headed for my bare toes; and then later, chases off a snapping turtle sunning in the mud. What next, I have to ask, an alligator?

Before he can prove himself with a mean critter the likes of that, we hear three rings of a bell around the bend.

We hurry on ahead and see a steamboat about to pull into a dock. The dock's piled with barrels, bales of cotton, and stacks of cut wood. There's a gathering of men and boys waving their arms, motioning the boat in.

Once again, civilization's staring us in the face.

The trick now is to get past the dock without being noticed or bothered.

—Stay close and act normal-like.

I walk with the air of a person who ain't scared of nothing. With me in these clothes, we might just pass for a normal boy and his normal dog wading and fishing.

We mosey up the river, the dog sniffing the edge of the water and me casting my spear now and then.

When we get close enough, I find us a rock to sit on, and we steal a good look at the steamboat.

Her name is written in big letters on the side wheel cover: *The Buzzard*.

I got to say, *The Buzzard* ain't the gleaming palace we saw last night. Her paint's peeling off and she looks pretty rickety, swaying at the edge of the river. The men are loading her up with cut wood, barrels, and cotton bales. Their speech tells me they're Irish, like some of the traders at Bent's Fort.

The man who seems to be in charge hollers at them to take special care with the whiskey barrels. His bald scalp's so red, it looks hot enough to fry a fish.

Then he turns back to the boys, who all look a bit older than me and are standing around like they're waiting for something.

—Now, boys, you see these rousters got a lot to haul before sundown. You help them get it all on board, and whichever ten of you work the hardest can go upriver with us.

The boys all scramble to the barrels and bales. Did I hear right? If they do good, they get to go upriver on the steamboat?

I look at the dog.

—You reckon I could pass for one of those boys?

He gives me a lazy look, like *Why not?*

Before I can think about it and get scared, I stand up, tilt my hat down, and hook my thumbs into my trouser pockets.

The dog wants to come with me, but I stop him.

—Stay here. I got to git us a job.

He looks grieved.

—Guard our things. I'll be back.

I leave my bag of possibles with him and keep walking. I'm lucky my new clothes hide the cuts on my arms and legs, and my hat hides my wild Indian hair. For once it's a good thing I got a plain face. A pretty girl wouldn't have a shot passing for one of those ugly boys.

I head across the dock toward the cotton bales.

—Hold on there.

The bald man's glaring at me.

—You're awful small.

I scowl at him and shrug.

—Well, go on. Try 'n' help haul those bales on to the main deck, near the bow.

As I copy the big boys, I pray my new genius for playacting will get me through the day. We roll the bales of cotton end over end across the swaying plank, on to the deck of *The Buzzard*.

I move as fast as I can. I work like the devil's in me, never stopping to joke with the others or wash my face in the river. I just keep delivering the bales on board, and the rousters stack them tier upon tier, until they reach all the way up to the highest deck.

When we finish with the cotton bales, I help tote wood to the furnace room. You'd never guess I'd about died a few days ago. I know if I do good work, me and the dog can ride upriver on the boat. That's what makes me work without stopping until sunset, when I drop in a faint.

The bald man splashes a bucket of river water on my head. When my eyes pop open, the dog is there licking my face.

I sit up and quickly pull my hat back on to hide my chopped hair. The bald man grins at me.

—You're a good worker, sonny, but you don't have to kill yourself. If you want to go upriver, you're hired. Half-dollar a day to help fuel the furnaces on the way, then help us unload when we get to Kansas Landing.

Kansas Landing. The sound of those words hits me like an earthquake. That's the very place I want to be! I can't believe my good luck!

I nod.

—Good. We leave at sunup. Tell your folks you'll be back in about two weeks.

I nod again, afraid to show my happiness. This is the best thing that's happened to me in my whole life!

I slowly stand up. I'm sore all over. But I try to keep steady on my feet as I walk off to get my bag of possibles.

Just as I'm about to pick it up, the bald man says one last thing.

—Oh, leave your dog home tomorrow, sonny. Captain don't allow no critters on the boat. If he finds him, he'll just throw him overboard.

We're camped a-ways from the levee. He's sound asleep, lying on his side, snoring the way he does.

I feel like the Great Holy Spirit is playing the Game of Hand with me. That's the game where your opponent holds a small stone in his hand and changes it back and forth behind his back, then holds out both hands and asks you to guess which one holds the stone.

Imagine the stone stands for doing what's right. Then you have to ask: is the stone in the hand that goes on the boat? Or the one that don't desert the dog? I won't know till I choose. And once I choose it'll be too late to change my mind.

If I choose to go on the steamboat to Kansas Landing, I'll hook up with a fur caravan heading back to Bent's Fort, so I can get there before winter comes.

If I choose to stay with him, we'll have to keep wandering on foot, eat what we can forage, sleep in the brush as the nights get colder, and try to stay out of sight. If it takes a week for the boat to get to Kansas Landing, it'd take at least a month walking. Can we make it? Everything tells me no.

I've run plumb into the reason Pa said never take a dog on the trail. You get to caring about him and risk your whole future. That's not the way of a good scout. Why, Pa didn't even let *me* stand in the way of *his* future.

I can't get no help from my ma, neither. Even if she could talk to me, I don't think she'd say, *Stay with the dog*. The Arapaho have a hundred dogs, and none's too special. Some even get eaten.

I can't imagine this ugly little mongrel would taste good. Funny thing about him, though, he don't stink like most do. It's a fact. When I lie down close to him right now and put my arm around him, his fur smells like the wild grass on the prairies.

I got to leave him. That's the choice I got to make. The hand opens – the stone's there. The steamboat's the only way I'll ever get back to the fort.

I ain't ever going to make a good scout if I'm fool enough to cry over him. Why, all the traders at the fort would laugh their heads off if they could see me now, crying like a baby into the sweet-smelling fur of a no-count dog, then sobbing even harder when he twists around to lick my tears.

I hold him tighter. Pa says if the Pawnees attack you on the prairie, their feathers and whoops put panic in your horses, so you have to tie the critters tight together, head to head in a circle to keep them from going mad.

Our heads is tight together now. As he goes back to sleep, he kicks his hind legs the way he does. He must be dreaming of our wanderings. I wonder, will he still dream of me when I'm gone?

I wake when it's barely light. *The Buzzard*'s going

to sail soon. The bald man said they'd be leaving at sun-up.

As I stand, the dog stretches to greet the day, then sneezes.

I don't look at him as I pull on my moccasins, brush off my clothes, and put on my hat.

I'm mad at him, mad because he's no good at taking care of himself. He don't seem to know how to hunt game. He can't even catch fish by himself! How's he ever going to get up the river without me to lead him?

—Listen. You got to start taking care of yourself.

But he won't. I know he won't. Right now he's looking at me like he's waiting for me to get us breakfast.

—Learn to feed yourself, dang fool!

I have to yell at him because he's such a fool. He's just an ugly little mongrel.

—Do you think you're a baby?

He smiles like I'm joking.

—You ain't a person.

Then I turn away. That ugly critter has got to

142

learn to feed himself. I ain't even going to look at him again. I have to go catch the boat. If I don't, I'll never get back to Bent's Fort and Indian country.

As I move down the bank, a hole's burning through my belly. But I ain't staying with him. This is the way I see it: my pa left me. He didn't even tell the Pathfinder about me. My ma left me, too. She lived for a while in my doll, but then disappeared and refused to come back. Who can blame folks for deserting an ugly mongrel?

Durn if he ain't right at my heels.

I whirl around and stare him in the eye, like a mean scout who ain't going to let hisself turn into a crybaby. I pretend to be my pa, cool and flinty-eyed.

—Git.

But the dog sneezes and wags his tail, like he thinks this is just another day on the river, and we're about to have some fun.

He ain't going to talk me into staying.

I turn back around, disgusted at us both. I ain't going to look at him again.

In fact, I'm starting to run from him. I limp as I run because my body's stiff and aching bad from loading the wood and cotton bales, but I keep going. I've *got* to catch the boat. It's taking me to my future.

When I look back, I see him running after me. I never saw such a dang fool.

—Leave me alone!

I shake my fist at him, and durn if I don't start to cry again. I could kill him for making me cry. I can't cry when I climb aboard *The Buzzard*. I got to be a tough boy who can work on a steamboat.

—Git, you!

I pick up a stick and hurl it at him.

—Leave me alone!

He stops running and sits still, like he does when he's confused. He just stares after me, looking worried-like.

—I hate you!

And I do because I love him, and he ain't coming with me.

—The captain'll throw you overboard, you stupid dog.

I have to go, or I'll never get back home, ever.

I start running, limping and stumbling away from him as fast as I can. But it ain't necessary. He don't try to follow. When I look back again, I see him just sitting there in the distance, an ugly little mongrel, staring sad-like.

And I hate him so much I could die.

When I get to the levee, soldiers and rivermen are already boarding *The Buzzard*, along with a few ladies in feathered bonnets and men in tall black hats. The boys and rousters I worked with yesterday are carrying sacks of rice and barrels of whiskey and soap on to the lower deck.

I catch sight of the bald man overseeing the loading, and he sees me, too.

—Hurry up, sonny, you're late! All hands take freight!

I drop my bag of possibles on the wooden landing and try to lift a sack of rice. When I get nowheres with that, I give up and begin rolling a whiskey barrel over the plank on to the boat.

I keep pushing the dog out of my mind. I ain't going to worry about him.

I get one barrel on board and go after another. I roll barrel after barrel like I'm rolling for my life. I don't know how many I wrestle across the slippery plank, but I don't stop till the levee's empty and the bald man shouts, She's ready to float!

I grab my bag and jump aboard with the boys. Four men pole the boat away from the shore.

—Woodpile, boys! Help the stokers!

I follow the boys to the dark, hot room where the furnaces are getting fired up. We pull green pine logs from the wood boxes and give them to the stokers.

More and more wood gets thrown in, until the fires are burning so hot it seems they could set the whole Missouri afire. At the very least, all of us.

I'm happy to be working hard because it keeps me from thinking and worrying.

The bell clangs on the hurricane deck. Then there's sputtering and wheezing. The whole boat trembles and shakes as her side wheels start to churn the water.

Some of the boys slip out of the room, but I stay on to help cram the fireboxes. My hands get black with soot, and I imagine my face does, too. But I don't mind. It makes me feel like I belong with the men doing the hard work of making the fire to make the steam to make the boat go upriver.

I work for hours, only stopping now and then for a drink from the water barrel they have for us.

Finally one of the deckhands hollers, Grub pile! Then he puts down a few pans filled with what looks like other folks' leftovers – pieces of bread, boiled potatoes, and chunks of meat. The stokers and me claw through the pans like starving cats.

When we get back to the fires, I work even harder than before. If thoughts of the dog cross my mind, I shove them off by picking up another piece of wood and passing it off to the firemen.

Git behind me, grief. It's my future I'm working for now.

But grief don't go away just like that. Grief nips at your heels, and if you think you've outrun it, you'll find grief waiting for you on the cargo deck when you hide there after dark. Grief ripples in the silver water and grief slips between the moonlit trees on the riverbank and grief rings in the fiddle music coming from the dance saloon above.

And when the stars shine bright, and you're trying to sleep between the cotton bales, grief's there, too. Look up at the sky, and you'll feel like grief is infinite, stretching out for ever, past the speckles of light into the unknown.

The dog is gone from my life now, alone and lost downriver somewhere. My pa broke his word to me and I don't know where Ma is any more. My book about the Heavenly Bodies has forced me to face the fact that she ain't up in the sky. There ain't no Land-Behind-the-Stars.

The night I was born, the knowledge of Science saved my life. It kept Running-in-a-Circle from killing me when Doc Hempstead explained about falling stars.

But now Science has banished my ma's spirit to a place I'll never know about. Science might even say she don't have a spirit. It might say her ashes is blowing somewhere near Horse Creek and that's all that's left of her, now and for ever more. And I feel quite sure Science would say there was no good reason to kill her white horse.

It seems the knowledge of Science can save your life. But at the same time, you have to ask, what for?

Why's life worth living, if everything you ever loved can turn to ashes and blow away?

All I know is, life seemed worth something when I was with that dog. Getting our food, healing my wounds, escaping the bear – it all seemed worth doing with him.

But Science would say he's just a dog, just a mongrel critter. Not important enough for that kind of human feeling. Not important enough for hardly any feelings at all.

—*Adaline Falling Star.*

Who said that?

—*Adaline Falling Star.*

There it goes again. Who's talking? It's not my ma. She only called me Falling Star. It's not my pa; he only calls me Adaline.

—*Go back for him.*

What?

—*Go back for him.*

I look up at the stars, at the speckles of light sprinkling into the unknown. It's me talking, the spirit of me, invisible to the eye of Science. And I know for sure what I have to do.

Forget Science. I have to go back for the dog.

I sit on my cotton bale, clutching my bag to my heart, waiting for the sun to rise.

Come fast, daybreak, and I'll find him, I promise. First levee we come to, I'll jump off the boat and search up and down the riverbank. Even if it takes for ever and three days, I'll find him.

But what makes me think he's still on the riverbank? He could have been drowned by now or bit by a snake. He could have taken off through the woods and been caught in a trap or shot by hunters, killed by a bear or a pack of wolves.

As it starts to get light, I can see the black smoke billowing from the steamboat's chimneys. Showers of sparks stream out with the smoke, and little pieces of fire float down to the deck.

You got to worry a bit about the cotton bales

catching fire. The whiskey barrels, too. Once, during a fire at Bent's Fort, a couple of whiskey barrels exploded, spraying the flaming liquor everywhere. A trapper named Dan Pawley got himself burned to death.

But as the sun starts to rise, red and glowing over the river, you can hardly see the sparks any more and it's easy to forget about them. Instead, I worry some more about the dog.

In the sunlight, the river seems so proud and important, I imagine a little dog means no more to her than a frog or a mud turtle.

When I get off the boat, I'll start walking south along the edge of the water, keeping my eyes skinned for the critter. I'll use all my scouting skills and all my Arapaho knowledge.

I keep seeing him sitting there, worried-like, watching me run off. And I try to quick shake off the picture. I can't stand to think about how I left him behind to be bear meat.

I jump off my cotton bale. I'm going to help the stokers again. The faster the fireboxes get fed, the faster we'll get to the next landing.

When I slip into the furnace room, I find everybody already at work. There's a stormy feeling in the air. I can't explain why, but some of the boys are talking and laughing in a strange way.

I line up with them. As we pass the pine logs to the stokers, some of the boys start acting rough. They yell at the rest of us to hurry up. They say they're tired of being on such a slow wreck.

When one shouts near my face, I smell liquor. I figure some of them must have got into the whiskey barrels during the night, and the liquor's what's making them wild.

At first the stokers think the boys are funny, but then the man in charge hollers at them to calm down.

The boys ignore him, and to make matters worse, a couple of them roll soap barrels into the furnace room and rip the barrels open and start hurling the soap into the fireboxes. The soap fat makes the fire roar like a tornado.

Now all the stokers start hollering at them. The boss grabs a boy and throws him out.

—We ain't having no racing here!

This kicks off a fight, a big fight, between the boys and the stokers.

In the red-hot glow of the roaring fire, the room's going crazy with yelling, cursing, and brawling. A couple of boys heave more soap fat into the fireboxes and one ties down the safety valve.

I'm not fighting, but I'm getting pushed around pretty bad. I slip and fall. Before I'm crushed to death, I grab my bag and crawl to the door.

One of the boys grabs my arm and pulls me back into the room, but I bite his hand. He hollers and swings his fist. I duck, then dash away.

Clutching my bag, I scramble up the stairs. I got to find somebody to stop the fight before something awful happens.

When I get to the hurricane deck, I catch sight of the captain standing near the bell. He's looking through his spyglass at something on the riverbank.

I holler at him.

—Fight in the fire room!

He looks at me funny, like he don't know who I am. But then he shouts to a couple of deckhands, and they all rush past me and head down the steps.

155

I stumble to the railing and lean against it to steady myself. As I'm standing there, trying to get my breath back, I see something in the distance, on the bank.

What is it?

It looks like a badger or maybe a groundhog running along the edge of the water. I squint my eyes and stand on tiptoe to see better.

The critter's running through the weeds, then under the cottonwoods and through the shadows. Then it's on the sand; then it's in the weeds again.

I move down the deck, clutching the railing. My eyes are staring so hard, I don't even blink. I can't really see the critter good enough to see what kind it is.

I run over and grab the captain's spyglass. As I fiddle with it to get a close view, my heart is thumping hard. It ain't pumping with fear from the fight, but rather from a surge of joy firing through my veins.

When I get a good look through the spyglass, my eyes catch sight of what my heart already knows. Joy courses right up through my throat and out my mouth.

—Dog! *Dog!*

The little critter freezes and stares at the boat. It feels like he's looking straight into my eyes. Ain't no doubt. It's *him!*

I just about lose my mind, jumping up and down, clutching the captain's spyglass. He's found his way back to me! He's the *true* Pathfinder! Look, ye saints! The sight is glorious!

But I stop celebrating when I see him leap over a log and start to wade into the river.

—No, fool!

The steamboat could roll right over him! Plus he ain't that good a swimmer.

As he starts swimming out to the boat, I holler at him.

—Go back! I'm coming to git you!

I put down the spyglass and pull off my moccasins and my hat. I leave my bag on the deck, say goodbye to *The Heavenly Bodies*, then climb up on the railing and point my hands down towards the ripply water. I take a deep breath and dive through the air till I crash headfirst into the river.

I plunge down deep into the muddy water, then bob up to the surface, gasping for air. I spit out a mouthful of river, then start swimming away from the boat.

I swim as fast as I can towards the dog, like when I paddled away from the bear.

Arm over arm over arm, I'm swimming away from my ride home, away from Bent's Fort, away from Indian country. I might never get back to all that. But all I want now is to be with the dog. I'm giving up my future and my old life, too, for this one thing I love.

Far behind me, men on the steamboat shout, Fire! Fire! I hear the bell clang and people screaming.

But I don't even look back. I just keep going, leaving everything behind.

I hear people splashing into the water. But I keep swimming, pointing myself straight at the dog.

His muskrat head is poking out above the river as he swims straight toward me.

The bell clangs and clangs.

Then the whole world blows up.

When I look back, I see a great cloud of smoke

and balls of fire shooting up into the sky.

The Buzzard keeps exploding. It sounds like a hundred rifles and cannons firing. With each blast, burning pieces of cotton and wood and metal fly into the air. Barrel slats and red-hot coals.

Some of the wreckage splashes down near me.

But I turn back to the dog and keep swimming. Can't nothing stop me now.

Then something hits me hard, smack on the forehead, right above my eye. I nearly black out and start to go under.

But I fight. Fight drowning. Fight losing him. I keep splashing my arms and moving my legs. Can't see but keep going. Use all my strength to keep above water. Swimming towards him. Blood streams down my face. Can't see. Keep going. Nothing can stop me. Keep going till we swim into each other. Clutch fur. Crawl out of the river. Fall on the sand. In my arms. Won't let him go. Blood everywhere. Screaming, hollering. Hold him tight. Mountains of smoke. Daylight turns to night again. Bits of fire fall through black sky. Stars raining down like the night I was born.

☆ ☆ ☆

Doc Hempstead is playing his squeaky violin. I stand under a tree in the morning mist. A young Arapaho girl is breaking off branches for her family's fire. A handsome trapper is chasing wild horses down from the hills.

The girl vanishes into the sky in a swirl of blue smoke, and the trapper can't find her. He sees me instead and uses his hands to ask if I'm an Indian girl? A white boy? Or a beautiful bird?

I answer I'm a beautiful bird. I tell him that me and Caddie use the sacred power of my eagle feather to soar to unseen heights. And in the next moment, we're doing just that, while Cousin Lilly runs below us, shaking a rag at the sky, screaming that she's going to scrub the stain out of us. But we sail past her and over John C. Fremont, who's arrived in St Louis, wearing his blue uniform with the gold braid. He don't see me flying with Caddie. He don't see her turn into my corn-husk doll . . . then into the dog.

Now it's the two of us, me and the dog riding to our freedom, high over the hills to the Land-Behind-the-Stars. We're riding on the back of my ma's white horse. When he comes to a stop, me and the dog tumble off his back on to a soft, white cloud. My ma picks me up and we start to dance with ghostly warriors in a golden circle as the sun rises above us. But while we're dancing, nobody notices the sky's getting hotter and hotter. John C. Fremont's heaving soap fat on to the sun. My part of the cloud starts to melt and I start to slip down, down through it. I scream for help, but no sound comes out. None of the dancers, including my ma, sees me falling through the cloud. I'm worried about the dog slipping through, too, but I can't find him. I'm desperate to find him. Before I can, I slip through the soft feathery whiteness, down through the blackness, down through lonely darkness, till I splash into a cold river. I crawl bleeding and bruised on to the shore, and the dog's there – I found him! He starts to lick my face, licking, licking, and licking. . .

—Hold on there.

I feel my face getting licked now and hear a dog whining and moaning.

—It's OK, she's gonna live.

I hear more whining, like the critter's gone mad from grief.

—There, there. You can sit on the bed close to her, but don't lick her to death.

I feel something furry press against my cheek. I smell the wild grass on the prairies.

I feel a big hand spread itself gentle-like over one of my hands. Then there's no more talking. Just the sounds of a man sniffling and blowing his nose.

By-and-by it grows quiet.

And I don't know for sure what's been real and what's been dreaming.

—There now. It's off.

I feel a breeze against my eyes. The top of my head feels naked. I wish for my hat.

—Adaline?

—Wait, let me wash her face.

It's a woman's voice.

A warm wet rag moves over my mouth, my cheeks and nose, then brushes against my eyelids.

—I'll leave you alone with her now.

I can't see anything at first. Only light and dark shapes. Then I breathe in the smell of leather and pipe tobacco.

—Adaline?

My vision starts to clear a bit. . . In the candlelight, I see a rough tanned face, sandy hair, and blue eyes.

I reach up and run my fingers slow-like down Pa's nose, across the worn hollows of his cheeks, and over his beard.

He gently takes hold of my hand and puts his mouth against it and kisses it long and hard. Then he sighs.

—Hey, darter.

His eyes are sad. They stop me from wanting to twist his ears and demand the truth.

Instead of sounding fierce-like, my voice is

weak and hoarse when I talk to him.

—Why ain't you in New Mexico?

—I was there. I bought us a ranch, then I come to git you. The slave woman told me the story what happened. I was looking on the river for you when I heard 'bout the steamboat, heard they'd found a girl nobody could name.

—I thought you broke your promise. I thought you weren't coming back for me.

Pa shakes his head, disgusted-like. He curls his fist around my hand and squeezes hard.

—I tole you I'd come for you. Give you my word. And you give me yours you'd wait, remember?

I just stare at him for a long moment. The truth is, Pa had come back for me. I was the one who'd broke our promise. Not him.

I nod.

—I remember.

But it don't seem he's too mad about it. In fact, he don't seem mad at all.

—What happened to the other folks on the boat? They get killed?

He nods.

—Some did. The ones what didn't jump in the river.

—I saw the dog – that's why I jumped – it was him what saved me.

—This ugly feller here?

Pa leans down and picks the dog up off the floor and puts him on the bed. Right away the critter sets to working on my ear and my cheek. His licking tickles me, making me laugh till I can get my hands around his face.

Then we just stare at each other in the candlelight, nose to nose. He's smiling like he does, and I have to say, his breath ain't no better than it ever was. I whisper in his ear.

—I ain't going to leave you again.

I look at Pa.

—He has to come with us, Pa. He saved my life.

A scowl crosses Pa's face. Then he nods.

—I reckon that'll be OK.

I turn back to the dog.

—You hear? You're coming with us. You like that?

His tongue hangs out, like he couldn't like it more if he tried.

Pa scratches the dog's ear. Then he looks back at me.

—You're going to like our new home. Taos, New Mexico. I bought us a piece of land on the Cimarron River.

—What about Bent's Fort? What about Horse Creek and Running-in-a-Circle?

Pa squints hard at me and shakes his head.

—Running-in-a-Circle got sick and died, Adaline. Ain't no Arapaho livin' on Horse Creek any more. Cholera got 'em.

I can't hardly bear to let this sink in – all my ma's people gone?

Somehow, though, I think I knew it already. I saw it in my vision when I had the fever – the dry wind blowing over scorched bones.

I picture Running-in-a-Circle riding his horse on the ghost trail.

—I wonder if he found Ma.

Pa takes a deep breath before he answers.

—I reckon he did. And I reckon he was real happy to see her.

Neither of us says anything else for a long moment. But when Pa stands up to leave, I know it's time to ask him one more question.

—Pa?

—Yep?

—How come you never told John C. Fremont about me?

He stares hard at me, like he's thinking about his answer. After a spell, he clears his throat.

—Truth is, I've never talked much to nobody about the things I love.

We hold each other's eyes for a moment. Then he looks away, bashful-like.

—It's late, darter. You better git some sleep.

The Pa I'm looking at is right smaller than the Pa I got in my heart. But the fact is, I love them both.

He leans over and kisses me on my forehead. Then he straightens up and brushes his hand over my hair. He pats the dog on the head, then blows out the light and leaves the room.

The dog and I are left alone together in the dark. I put my arm around his skinny body, and he licks my cheek.

Men like Pa might not talk about the things they love. But I'm different, way different. When I'm on the trail I'll talk about my pa and my ma. I'll talk about Running-in-a-Circle and Caddie. And I'll talk about this dog. All my life I'll talk about him. I'll tell the moon and the stars about him, I'll tell anyone who'll listen, tell them how he saved me from drowning the first day we met, how he saved me from fever and saved me from fire.

And if someone says, Aw, that fool dog would have taken up just as easy with anybody who happened to cross his path, I'll say it ain't so. We're a match; we're both mongrels. He's got all kinds of critter in him, might even be part muskrat. I love him for his mix, and he loves me for mine.

He sits closer to me and I press my cheek against his prairie-smelling fur, and we stare together out the window at the night sky, at all the stars sprinkled throughout the unknown.